*The Gerrard Street Mystery
and Other Weird Tales*

John Charles Dent

Contents

THE GERRARD STREET MYSTERY

AND OTHER WEIRD TALES

BY

John Charles Dent

PREFATORY SKETCH.

John Charles Dent, the author of the following remarkable stories, was born in Kendal, Westmorland, England, in 1841. His parents emigrated to Canada shortly after that event, bringing with them, of course, the youth who was afterwards to become the Canadian author and historian. Mr. Dent received his primary education in Canadian schools, and afterwards studied law, becoming in due course a member of the Upper Canada Bar. He only practised for a few years. He found the profession profitable enough but uncongenial--as it could not well help being, in an obscure Canadian, village, twenty years ago--and very probably he was already cherishing ambitious dreams of literary labors, which he was eager to begin in the world's literary centre, London. He accordingly relinquished his practice as soon as he felt himself in a position to do so, and went to England. He had not miscalculated his powers, as too many do under like circumstances. He soon found remunerative literary work, and as he became better known, was engaged to write for several high-class periodicals, notably, **Once a Week**, for which he contributed a series of articles on interesting topics. But in England Mr. Dent produced no very long or ambitious work. Perhaps he found that the requisite time for such an undertaking could not be spared. At this period he had a wife and family depending on him for support, and it speaks well for his abilities, that he was able to amply provide for them out of the profits solely derived from his literary labours. But of course to do this he had to devote himself to work that could be thrown off readily, and which could be as readily sold.

After remaining in England for several years, Mr. Dent and his family returned to America. He obtained a position in Boston, which he held for about two years. But he finally relinquished it and came to Toronto, having accepted a position on the editorial staff of the **Telegram**, which was then just starting. For several years

Mr. Dent devoted himself to journalistic labours on various newspapers, but principally the **Toronto Weekly Globe**. To that journal he contributed a very notable series of biographical sketches on "Eminent Canadians." Shortly after the death of the Hon. George Brown, Mr. Dent severed his connection with the **Globe**, and immediately thereafter commenced his first ambitious undertaking, **The Canadian Portrait Gallery**, which ran to four large volumes. It proved to be a most creditable and successful achievement. Of course in a brief sketch no detailed criticism of either this or the succeeding works can be attempted. Suffice it to say that the biographies of Canadian public men, living and dead, were carefully prepared, and written from an un-partisan standpoint. In this book there was no padding; every individual admitted had achieved something of national value, and the biographies are, therefore, of importance to the student of Canadian history. This book deserved and attained a considerable circulation, and brought to its author a comparatively large sum of money.

Mr. Dent's second book was "The Last Forty Years: Canada since the Union of 1841." This work has been highly praised in all quarters, and is in every way a credit to its author's really brilliant powers as a literary artist.

The third work was a "History of the Rebellion in Upper Canada." Although written in his best manner, with the greatest possible care, from authentic sources of information not hitherto accessible, this work has had the misfortune to meet with undeservedly severe criticism. When Mr. Dent began his studies for the book he held William-Lyon Mackenzie in high esteem, but he found it necessary afterwards to change his opinion. He was able to throw a flood of new light on the characters of the men who took part in the struggle, and if the facts tended to darken the fair fame of some of them, the historian certainly ought not to be censured for it. The tendency of the book was decidedly in opposition to the ideas entertained to this day by the partizans of the "Old Family Compact" on the one side, and also to the friends and admirers of William Lyon Mackenzie on the other.

But the severe criticism the work sustained, has left it stronger than before, and it will stand undoubtedly as by far the best history of the "Rebellion" that has appeared.

In addition to these important works on which his reputation as a writer will rest, Mr. Dent has written from time to time a great many sketches, essays and stories, some of which are exceedingly interesting and worthy of being preserved. All of Mr. Dent's work contains a charm of its own. In writing, history, he was in accord with Macaulay. He always believed that a true story should be told as agreeably as a fictitious one; "that the incidents of real life, whether political or domestic, admit of being so arranged as, without detriment to accuracy, to command all the interest of an artificial series of facts; that the chain of circumstances which constitute history may be as finely and gracefully woven as any tale of fancy." Acting upon this theory, he has made Canadian history very interesting reading. He is to my mind the only historian, beside Mr. Parkman, who has been able to make Canadian events so dry in detail, fascinating throughout.

In private life, Mr. Dent was a most estimable man. He possessed qualities of mind and heart, having their visible outcome in a courteous, genial manner that endeared him very closely to his friends. With all his wealth of learning, which was very great, he was light-hearted, witty and companionable, and his early death leaves a gap not very easily closed.

The four stories composing the present volume were contributed by their author at considerable intervals to different periodicals. Some time prior to his death he contemplated publishing them in book form, and actually selected and carefully revised them with that purpose in view. He thought they were worthy of being rescued from obscurity, and if we compare them with much of a similar class of work constantly issuing from the press, we cannot think that his judgment erred. They are now published in accordance with his wish, to take their chances in the great world of literature.

R. W. D.

TORONTO, Oct. 25th, 1888.

THE GERRARD STREET MYSTERY.
I.

My name is William Francis Furlong. My occupation is that of a commission merchant, and my place of business is on St. Paul Street, in the City of Montreal. I have resided in Montreal ever since shortly after my marriage, in 1862, to my cousin, Alice Playter, of Toronto. My name may not be familiar to the present generation of Torontonians, though I was born in Toronto, and passed the early years of my life there. Since the days of my youth my visits to the Upper Province have been few, and--with one exception--very brief; so that I have doubtless passed out of the remembrance of many persons with whom I was once on terms of intimacy. Still, there are several residents of Toronto whom I am happy to number among my warmest personal friends at the present day. There are also a good many persons of middle age, not in Toronto only, but scattered here and there throughout various parts of Ontario, who will have no difficulty in recalling my name as that of one of their fellow-students at Upper Canada College. The name of my late uncle, Richard Yardington, is of course well known to all old residents of Toronto, where he spent the last thirty-two years of his life. He settled there in the year 1829, when the place was still known as Little York. He opened a small store on Yonge Street, and his commercial career was a reasonably prosperous one. By steady degrees the small store developed into what, in those times, was regarded as a considerable establishment. In the course of years the owner acquired a competency, and in 1854 retired from business altogether. From that time up to the day of his death he lived in his own house on Gerrard Street.

After mature deliberation, I have resolved to give to the Canadian public an account of some rather singular circumstances connected with my residence in Toronto. Though repeatedly urged to do so, I have hitherto refrained from giving any extended publicity to those circumstances, in consequence of my inability to see any good to be served thereby. The only person, however, whose reputation can be injuriously affected by the details has been dead for some years. He has left behind him no one whose feelings can be shocked by the disclosure, and the story is in itself sufficiently remarkable to be worth the telling. Told, accordingly, it shall be; and the only fictitious element introduced into the narrative shall be the name of one of the persons most immediately concerned in it.

At the time of taking up his abode in Toronto--or rather in Little York--my uncle Richard was a widower, and childless; his wife having died several months previously. His only relatives on this side of the Atlantic were two maiden sisters, a few years younger than himself. He never contracted a second matrimonial alliance, and for some time after his arrival here his sisters lived in his house, and were dependent upon him for support. After the lapse of a few years both of them married and settled down in homes of their own. The elder of them subsequently became my mother. She was left a widow when I was a mere boy, and survived my father only a few months. I was an only child, and as my parents had been in humble circumstances, the charge of my maintenance devolved upon my uncle, to whose kindness I am indebted for such educational training as I have received. After sending me to school and college for several years, he took me into his store, and gave me my first insight into commercial life. I lived with him, and both then and always received at his hands the kindness of a father, in which light I eventually almost came to regard him. His younger sister, who was married to a watchmaker called Elias Playter, lived at Quebec from the time of her marriage until her death, which took place in 1846. Her husband had been unsuccessful in business, and was moreover of dissipated habits. He was left with one child--a daughter--on his hands; and as my uncle was averse to the idea of his sister's child remaining under the control of one so unfit to provide for her welfare, he proposed to adopt the little girl as his own. To this proposition Mr. Elias Playter readily assented, and little Alice was soon domiciled with her uncle and myself in Toronto.

Brought up, as we were, under the same roof, and seeing each other every day of our lives, a childish attachment sprang up between my cousin Alice and myself. As the years rolled by, this attachment ripened into a tender affection, which eventually resulted in an engagement between us. Our engagement was made with the full and cordial approval of my uncle, who did not share the prejudice entertained by many persons against marriages between cousins. He stipulated, however, that our marriage should be deferred until I had seen somewhat more of the world, and until we had both reached an age when we might reasonably be presumed to know our own minds. He was also, not unnaturally, desirous that before taking upon myself the responsibility of marriage I should give some evidence of my ability to provide for a wife, and for other contingencies usually consequent upon matrimony. He made no secret of his intention to divide his property between Alice and myself at his death; and the fact that no actual division would be necessary in the event of our marriage with each other was doubtless one reason for his ready acquiescence in our engagement. He was, however, of a vigorous constitution, strictly regular and methodical in all his habits, and likely to live to an advanced age. He could hardly be called parsimonious, but, like most men who have successfully fought their own way through life, he was rather fond of authority, and little disposed to divest himself of his wealth until he should have no further occasion for it. He expressed his willingness to establish me in business, either in Toronto or elsewhere, and to give me the benefit of his experience in all mercantile transactions.

When matters had reached this pass I had just completed my twenty-first year, my cousin being three years younger. Since my uncle's retirement I had engaged in one or two little speculations on my own account, which had turned out fairly successful, but I had not devoted myself to any regular or fixed pursuit. Before any definite arrangements had been concluded as to the course of my future life, a circumstance occurred which seemed to open a way for me to turn to good account such mercantile talent as I possessed. An old friend of my uncle's opportunely arrived in Toronto from Melbourne, Australia, where, in the course of a few years, he had risen from the position of a junior clerk to that of senior partner in a prominent commercial house. He painted the land of his adoption in glowing colours, and assured my uncle and myself that it presented an inviting field for a young man of energy and business capacity, more especially if he had a small capital at his command. The matter was carefully debated in our domestic circle. I was naturally averse to a separation from Alice, but my imagination took fire at Mr. Redpath's glowing account of his own splendid success. I pictured myself returning to Canada after an absence of four or five years with a mountain of gold at my command, as the result of my own energy and acuteness. In imagination, I saw myself settled down with Alice in a palatial mansion on Jarvis Street, and living in affluence all the rest of my days. My uncle bade me consult my own judgment in the matter, but rather encouraged the idea than otherwise. He offered to advance me L500, and I had about half that sum as the result of my own speculations. Mr. Redpath, who was just about returning to Melbourne, promised to aid me to the extent of his power with his local knowledge and advice. In less than a fortnight from that time he and I were on our way to the other side of the globe.

We reached our destination early in the month of September, 1857. My life in Australia has no direct bearing upon the course of events to be related, and may be passed over in a very few words. I engaged in various enterprises, and achieved a certain measure of success. If none of my ventures proved eminently prosperous, I at least met with no serious disasters. At the end of four years--that is to say, in September, 1861--I made up my account with the world, and found I was worth ten thousand dollars. I had, however, become terribly homesick, and longed for the termination of my voluntary exile. I had, of course, kept up a regular correspondence with Alice and Uncle Richard, and of late they had both pressed me to return home. "You have enough," wrote my uncle, "to give you a start in Toronto, and I see no reason why Alice and you should keep apart any longer. You will have no housekeeping expenses, for I intend you to live with me. I am getting old, and shall be glad of your companionship in my declining years. You will have a comfortable home while I live, and when I die you will get all I have between you. Write as soon as you receive this, and let us know how soon you can be here,--the sooner the better."

The letter containing this pressing invitation found me in a mood very much disposed to accept it. The only enterprise I had on hand which would be likely to delay me was a transaction in wool, which, as I believed, would be closed by the end of January or the beginning of February. By the first of March I should certainly be in a condition to start on my homeward voyage, and I determined that my departure should take place about that time. I wrote both to Alice and my uncle, apprising them of my intention, and announcing my expectation to reach Toronto not later than the middle of May.

The letters so written were posted on the 19th of September, in time for the mail which left on the following day. On the 27th, to my huge surprise and gratification, the wool transaction referred to was unexpectedly concluded, and I was at liberty, if so disposed, to start for home by the next fast mail steamer, the **Southern Cross**, leaving Melbourne on the 11th of October. I **was** so disposed, and made my preparations accordingly. It was useless, I reflected, to write to my uncle or to Alice, acquainting them with the change in my plans, for I should take the shortest route home, and should probably be in Toronto as soon as a letter could get there. I resolved to telegraph from New York, upon my arrival there, so as not to take them altogether by surprise.

The morning of the 11th of October found me on board the **Southern Cross**, where I shook hands with Mr. Redpath and several other friends who accompanied me on board for a last farewell. The particulars of the voyage to England are not pertinent to the story, and may be given very briefly. I took the Red Sea route, and arrived at Marseilles about two o'clock in the afternoon of the 29th of November. From Marseilles I travelled by rail to Calais, and so impatient was I to reach my journey's end without loss of time, that I did not even stay over to behold the glories of Paris. I had a commission to execute in London, which, however, delayed me there only a few hours, and I hurried down to Liverpool, in the hope of catching the Cunard Steamer for New York. I missed it by about two hours, but the **Persia** was detailed to start on a special trip to Boston on the following day. I secured a berth, and at eight o'clock the next morning steamed out of the Mersey on my way homeward.

The voyage from Liverpool to Boston consumed fourteen days. All I need say about it is, that before arriving at the latter port I formed an intimate acquaintance with one of the passengers--Mr. Junius H. Gridley, a Boston merchant, who was returning from a hurried business trip to Europe. He was--and is--a most agreeable companion. We were thrown together a good deal during the voyage, and we then laid the foundation of a friendship which has ever since subsisted between us. Before the dome of the State House loomed in sight he had extracted a promise from me to spend a night with him before pursuing my journey. We landed at the wharf in East Boston on the evening of the 17th of December, and I accompanied him to his house on West Newton Street, where I remained until the following morning.

Upon consulting the time-table, we found that the Albany express would leave at 11.30 a.m. This left several hours at my disposal, and we sallied forth immediately after breakfast to visit some of the lions of the American Athens.

In the course of our peregrinations through the streets, we dropped into the post-office, which had recently been established in the Merchants' Exchange Building, on State Street. Seeing the countless piles of mail-matter, I jestingly remarked to my friend that there seemed to be letters enough there to go around the whole human family. He replied in the same mood, whereupon I banteringly suggested the probability that among so many letters, surely there ought to be one for me.

"Nothing more reasonable," he replied. "We Bostonians are always bountiful to strangers. Here is the General Delivery, and here is the department where letters addressed to the Furlong family are kept in stock. Pray inquire for yourself."

The joke I confess was not a very brilliant one; but with a grave countenance I stepped up to the wicket and asked the young lady in attendance:

"Anything for W. F. Furlong?"

She took from a pigeon-hole a handful of correspondence, and proceeded to run her eye over the addresses. When about half the pile had been exhausted she stopped, and propounded the usual inquiry in the case of strangers:

"Where do you expect letters from?"

"From Toronto," I replied.

To my no small astonishment she immediately handed me a letter, bearing the Toronto post-mark. The address was in the peculiar and well-known handwriting of my uncle Richard.

Scarcely crediting the evidence of my senses I tore open the envelope, and read as follows:--

"TORONTO, 9th December, 1861.

"MY DEAR WILLIAM--I am so glad to know that you are coming home so much sooner than you expected when you wrote last, and that you will eat your Christmas dinner with us. For reasons which you will learn when you arrive, it will not be a very merry Christmas at our house, but your presence will make it much more bearable than it would be without you. I have not told Alice that you are coming. Let it be a joyful surprise for her, as some compensation for the sorrows she has had to endure lately. You needn't telegraph. I will meet you at the G. W.

R. station.

    "Your affectionate uncle,   "RICHARD YARDINGTON."

    "Why, what's the matter?" asked my friend, seeing the blank look of surprise on my face. "Of course the letter is not for you; why on earth did you open it?"

    "It *is* for me," I answered. "See here, Gridley, old man; have you been playing me a trick? If you haven't, this is the strangest thing I ever knew in my life."

    Of course he hadn't been playing me a trick. A moment's reflection showed me that such a thing was impossible. Here was the envelope, with the Toronto post-mark of the 9th of December, at which time he had been with me on board the *Persia*, on the Banks of Newfoundland. Besides, he was a gentleman, and would not have played so poor and stupid a joke upon a guest. And, to put the matter beyond all possibility of doubt, I remembered that I had never mentioned my cousin's name in his hearing.

    I handed him the letter. He read it carefully through twice over, and was as much mystified at its contents as myself; for during our passage across the Atlantic I had explained to him the circumstance under which I was returning home.

    By what conceivable means had my uncle been made aware of my departure from Melbourne? Had Mr. Redpath written to him, as soon as I acquainted that gentleman with my intentions? But even if such were the case, the letter could not have left before I did, and could not possibly have reached Toronto by the 9th of December. Had I been seen in England by some one who knew me, and had not one written from there? Most unlikely; and even if such a thing had happened, it was impossible that the letter could have reached Toronto by the 9th. I need hardly inform the reader that there was no telegraphic communication at that time. And how could my uncle know that I would take the Boston route? And if he *had* known, how could he foresee that I would do anything so absurd as to call at the Boston post-office and inquire for letters? "*I will meet you at the G. W. R. station.*" How was he to know by what train I would reach Toronto, unless I notified him by telegraph? And that he expressly stated to be unnecessary.

    We did no more sight-seeing. I obeyed the hint contained in the letter, and sent no telegram. My friend accompanied me down to the Boston and Albany station, where I waited in feverish impatience for the departure of the train. We talked over the matter until 11.30, in the vain hope of finding some clue to the mystery.

Then I started on my journey. Mr. Gridley's curiosity was aroused, and I promised to send him an explanation immediately upon my arrival at home.

No sooner had the train glided out of the station than I settled myself in my seat, drew the tantalizing letter from my pocket, and proceeded to read and re-read it again and again. A very few perusals sufficed to fix its contents in my memory, so that I could repeat every word with my eyes shut. Still I continued to scrutinize the paper, the penmanship, and even the tint of the ink. For what purpose, do you ask? For no purpose, except that I hoped, in some mysterious manner, to obtain more light on the subject. No light came, however. The more I scrutinized and pondered, the greater was my mystification. The paper was a simple sheet of white letter-paper, of the kind ordinarily used by my uncle in his correspondence. So far as I could see, there was nothing peculiar about the ink. Anyone familiar with my uncle's writing could have sworn that no hand but his had penned the lines. His well-known signature, a masterpiece of involved hieroglyphics, was there in all its indistinctness, written as no one but himself could ever have written it. And yet, for some unaccountable reason, I was half disposed to suspect forgery. Forgery! What nonsense. Anyone clever enough to imitate Richard Yardington's handwriting would have employed his talents more profitably than indulging in a mischievous and purposeless jest. Not a bank in Toronto but would have discounted a note with that signature affixed to it.

Desisting from all attempts to solve these problems, I then tried to fathom the meaning of other points in the letter. What misfortune had happened to mar the Christmas festivities at my uncle's house? And what could the reference to my cousin Alice's sorrows mean? She was not ill. *That*, I thought, might be taken for granted. My uncle would hardly have referred to her illness as "one of the sorrows she had to endure lately." Certainly, illness may be regarded in the light of a sorrow; but "sorrow" was not precisely the word which a straight-forward man like Uncle Richard would have applied to it. I could conceive of no other cause of affliction in her case. My uncle was well, as was evinced by his having written the letter, and by his avowed intention to meet me at the station. Her father had died long before I started for Australia. She had no other near relation except myself, and she had no cause for anxiety, much less for "sorrow," on my account. I thought it singular, too, that my uncle, having in some strange manner become acquainted with my movements, had withheld the knowledge from Alice. It did not square with my preconceived ideas of him that he would derive any satisfaction from taking his niece by surprise.

All was a muddle together, and as my temples throbbed with the intensity of my thoughts, I was half disposed to believe myself in a troubled dream from which I should presently awake. Meanwhile, on glided the train.

A heavy snow-storm delayed us for several hours, and we reached Hamilton too late for the mid-day express for Toronto. We got there, however, in time for the accommodation leaving at 3.15 p.m., and we would reach Toronto at 5.05. I walked from one end of the train to the other in hopes of finding some one I knew, from whom I could make enquiries about home. Not a soul. I saw several persons whom I knew to be residents of Toronto, but none with whom I had ever been personally acquainted, and none of them would be likely to know anything about my uncle's domestic arrangements. All that remained to be done under these circumstances was to restrain my curiosity as well as I could until reaching Toronto. By the by, would my uncle really meet me at the station, according to his promise? Surely not. By what means could he possibly know that I would arrive by this train? Still, he seemed to have such accurate information respecting my proceedings that there was no saying where his knowledge began or ended. I tried not to think about the matter, but as the train approached Toronto my impatience became positively feverish in its intensity. We were not more than three minutes behind time, as we glided in front of the Union Station, I passed out on to the platform of the car, and peered intently through the darkness. Suddenly my heart gave a great bound. There, sure enough, standing in front of the door of the waiting-room, was my uncle, plainly discernible by the fitful glare of the overhanging lamps. Before the train came to a stand-still, I sprang from the car and advanced towards him. He was looking out for me, but his eyes not being as young as mine, he did not recognize me until I grasped him by the hand. He greeted me warmly, seizing me by the waist, and almost raising me from the ground. I at once noticed several changes in his appearance; changes for which I was wholly unprepared. He had aged very much since I had last seen him, and the lines about his mouth had deepened considerably. The iron-grey hair which I remembered so well had disappeared; its place being supplied with a new and rather dandified-looking wig. The oldfashioned great-coat which he had worn ever since I could remember had been supplanted by a modern frock of spruce cut, with seal-skin collar and cuffs. All this I noticed in the first hurried greetings that passed between us.

"Never mind your luggage, my boy," he remarked. "Leave it till to-morrow, when we will send down for it. If you are not tired we'll walk home instead of taking a cab. I have a good deal to say to you before we get there."

I had not slept since leaving Boston, but was too much excited to be conscious of fatigue, and as will readily be believed, I was anxious enough to hear what he had to say. We passed from the station, and proceeded up York Street, arm in arm.

"And now, Uncle Richard," I said, as soon as we were well clear of the crowd,--"keep me no longer in suspense. First and foremost, is Alice well?"

"Quite well, but for reasons you will soon understand, she is in deep grief. You must know that--"

"But," I interrupted, "tell me, in the name of all that's wonderful, how you knew I was coming by this train; and how did you come to write to me at Boston?"

Just then we came to the corner of Front Street, where was a lamp-post. As we reached the spot where the light of the lamp was most brilliant, he turned half round, looked me full in the face, and smiled a sort of wintry smile. The expression of his countenance was almost ghastly.

"Uncle," I quickly said, "What's the matter? Are you not well?"

"I am not as strong as I used to be, and I have had a good deal to try me of late. Have patience and I will tell you all. Let us walk more slowly, or I shall not finish before we get home. In order that you may clearly understand how matters are, I had better begin at the beginning, and I hope you will not interrupt me with any questions till I have done. How I knew you would call at the Boston post-office, and that you would arrive in Toronto by this train, will come last in order. By the by, have you my letter with you?"

"The one you wrote to me at Boston? Yes, here it is," I replied, taking it from my pocket-book.

"Let me have it."

I handed it to him, and he put it into the breast pocket of his inside coat. I wondered at this proceeding on his part, but made no remark upon it.

We moderated our pace, and he began his narration. Of course I don't pretend to remember his exact words, but they were to this effect. During the winter following my departure to Melbourne, he had formed the acquaintance of a gentleman who had then recently settled in Toronto. The name of this gentleman was Marcus Weatherley, who had commenced business as a wholesale provision merchant immediately upon his arrival, and had been engaged in it ever since. For more than three years the acquaintance between him and my uncle had been very slight, but during the last summer they had had some real estate transactions together, and had become intimate. Weatherley, who was comparatively a young man and unmarried, had been invited to the house on Gerrard Street, where he had more recently become a pretty frequent visitor. More recently still, his visits had become so frequent that my uncle suspected him of a desire to be attentive to my cousin, and had thought proper to enlighten him as to her engagement with me. From that day his visits had been voluntarily discontinued. My uncle had not given much consideration to the subject until a fortnight afterwards, when he had accidently become aware of the fact that Weatherley was in embarrassed circumstances.

Here my uncle paused in his narrative to take breath. He then added, in a low tone, and putting his mouth almost close to my ear:

"And, Willie, my boy, I have at last found out something else. He has forty-two thousand dollars falling due here and in Montreal within the next ten days, and *he has forged my signature to acceptances for thirty-nine thousand seven hundred and sixteen dollars and twenty-four cents*."

Those to the best of my belief, were his exact words. We had walked up York Street to Queen, and then had gone down Queen to Yonge, when we turned up the east side on our way homeward. At the moment when the last words were uttered we had got a few yards north of Crookshank Street, immediately in front of a chemist's shop which was, I think, the third house from the corner. The window of this shop was well lighted, and its brightness was reflected on the sidewalk in front. Just then, two gentlemen walking rapidly in the opposite direction to that we were taking brushed by us; but I was too deeply absorbed in my uncle's communication to pay much attention to passers-by. Scarcely had they passed, however, ere one of them stopped and exclaimed:

"Surely that is Willie Furlong!"

I turned, and recognised Johnny Gray, one of my oldest friends. I relinquished my uncle's arm for a moment, and shook hands with Gray, who said:

"I am surprised to see you. I heard only a few days ago, that you were not to be here till next spring."

"I am here," I remarked, "somewhat in advance of my own expectations." I then hurriedly enquired after several of our common friends, to which enquiries he briefly replied.

"All well," he said; "but you are in a hurry, and so am I. Don't let me detain you. Be sure and look in on me to-morrow. You will find me at the old place, in the Romain Buildings."

We again shook hands, and he passed on down the street with the gentleman who accompanied him. I then turned to re-possess myself of my uncle's arm. The old gentleman had evidently walked on, for he was not in sight. I hurried along, making sure of overtaking him before reaching Gould Street, for my interview with Gray had occupied barely a minute. In another minute I was at the corner of Gould Street. No signs of Uncle Richard. I quickened my pace to a run, which soon brought me to Gerrard Street. Still no signs of my uncle. I had certainly not passed him on my way, and he could not have got farther on his homeward route than here. He must have called in at one of the stores; a strange thing for him to do under the circumstances. I retraced my steps all the way to the front of the chemist's shop, peering into every window and doorway as I passed along. No one in the least resembling him was to be seen.

I stood still for a moment, and reflected. Even if he had run at full speed--a thing most unseemly for him to do--he could not have reached the corner of Gerrard Street before I had done so. And what should he run for? He certainly did not wish to avoid me, for he had more to tell me before reaching home. Perhaps he had turned down Gould Street. At any rate, there was no use waiting for him. I might as well go home at once. And I did.

Upon reaching the old familiar spot, I opened the gate passed on up the steps to the front door, and rang the bell. The door was opened by a domestic who had not formed part of the establishment in my time, and who did not know me; but Alice happened to be passing through the hall, and heard my voice as I inquired for Uncle Richard. Another moment and she was in my arms. With a strange foreboding at my heart I noticed that she was in deep mourning. We passed into the dining-room, where the table was laid for dinner.

"Has Uncle Richard come in?" I asked, as soon as we were alone. "Why did he run away from me?"

"Who?" exclaimed Alice, with a start; "what do you mean, Willie? Is it possible you have not heard?"

"Heard what?"

"I see you have **not** heard," she replied. "Sit down, Willie, and prepare yourself for painful news. But first tell me what you meant by saying what you did just now,--who was it that ran away from you?"

"Well, perhaps I should hardly call it running away, but he certainly disappeared most mysteriously, down here near the corner of Yonge and Crookshank Streets."

"Of whom are you speaking?"

"Of Uncle Richard, of course."

"Uncle Richard! The corner of Yonge and Crookshank Streets! When did you see him there?"

"When? A quarter of an hour ago. He met me at the station and we walked up together till I met Johnny Gray. I turned to speak to Johnny for a moment, when--"

"Willie, what on earth are you talking about? You are labouring under some strange delusion. *Uncle Richard died of apoplexy more than six weeks ago, and lies buried in St. James's Cemetery.*"

II.

I don't know how long I sat there, trying to think, with my face buried in my hands. My mind had been kept on a strain during the last thirty hours, and the succession of surprises to which I had been subjected had temporarily paralyzed my faculties. For a few moments after Alice's announcement I must have been in a sort of stupor. My imagination, I remember, ran riot about everything in general, and nothing in particular. My cousin's momentary impression was that I had met with an accident of some kind, which had unhinged my brain. The first distinct remembrance I have after this is, that I suddenly awoke from my stupor to find Alice kneeling at my feet, and holding me by the hand. Then my mental powers came back to me, and I recalled all the incidents of the evening.

"When did uncle's death take place?" I asked.

"On the 3rd of November, about four o'clock in the afternoon. It was quite unexpected, though he had not enjoyed his usual health for some weeks before. He fell down in the hall, just as he was returning from a walk, and died within two hours. He never spoke or recognised any one after his seizure."

"What has become of his old overcoat?" I asked.

"His old overcoat, Willie--what a question?" replied Alice, evidently thinking that I was again drifting back into insensibility.

"Did he continue to wear it up to the day of his death?" I asked.

"No. Cold weather set in very early this last fall, and he was compelled to don his winter clothing earlier than usual. He had a new overcoat made within a fortnight before he died. He had it on at the time of his seizure. But why do you ask?"

"Was the new coat cut by a fashionable tailor, and had it a fur collar and cuffs?"

"It was cut at Stovel's, I think. It had a fur collar and cuffs."

"When did he begin to wear a wig?"

"About the same time that he began to wear his new overcoat. I wrote you a letter at the time, making merry over his youthful appearance and hinting--of course only in jest--that he was looking out for a young wife. But you surely did not receive my letter. You must have been on your way home before it was written."

"I left Melbourne on the 11th of October. The wig, I suppose, was buried with him?"

"Yes."

"And where is the overcoat?"

"In the wardrobe upstairs, in uncle's room."

"Come and show it to me."

I led the way upstairs, my cousin following. In the hall on the first floor we encountered my old friend Mrs. Daly, the housekeeper. She threw up her hands in surprise at seeing me. Our greeting was very brief; I was too intent on solving the problem which had exercised my mind ever since receiving the letter at Boston, to pay much attention to anything else. Two words, however, explained to her where we were going, and at our request she accompanied us. We passed into my uncle's room. My cousin drew the key of the wardrobe from a drawer where it was kept, and unlocked the door. There hung the overcoat. A single glance was sufficient. It was the same.

The dazed sensation in my head began to make itself felt again. The atmosphere of the room seemed to oppress me, and closing the door of the wardrobe, I led the way down stairs again to the dining-room, followed by my cousin. Mrs. Daly had sense enough to perceive that we were discussing family matters, and retired to her own room.

I took my cousin's hand in mine, and asked:

"Will you tell me what you know of Mr. Marcus Weatherley?"

This was evidently another surprise for her. How could I have heard of Marcus Weatherley? She answered, however, without hesitation:

"I know very little of him. Uncle Richard and he had some dealings a few months since, and in that way he became a visitor here. After a while he began to call pretty often, but his visits suddenly ceased a short time before uncle's death. I need not affect any reserve with you. Uncle Richard thought he came after me, and gave him a hint that you had a prior claim. He never called afterwards. I am rather glad that he didn't, for there is something about him that I don't quite like. I am at a loss to say what the something is; but his manner always impressed me with the idea that he was not exactly what he seemed to be on the surface. Perhaps I misjudged him. Indeed, I think I must have done so, for he stands well with everybody, and is highly respected."

I looked at the clock on the mantel piece. It was ten minutes to seven, I rose from my seat.

"I will ask you to excuse me for an hour or two, Alice. I must find Johnny Gray."

"But you will not leave me, Willie, until you have given me some clue to your unexpected arrival, and to the strange questions you have been asking? Dinner is ready, and can be served at once. Pray don't go out again till you have dined."

She clung to my arm. It was evident that she considered me mad, and thought it probable that I might make away with myself. This I could not bear. As for eating any dinner, that was simply impossible in my then frame of mind, although I had not tasted food since leaving Rochester. I resolved to tell her all. I resumed my seat. She placed herself on a stool at my feet, and listened while I told her all that I have set down as happening to me subsequently to my last letter to her from Melbourne.

"And now, Alice, you know why I wish to see Johnny Gray."

She would have accompanied me, but I thought it better to prosecute my inquiries alone. I promised to return sometime during the night, and tell her the result of my interview with Gray. That gentleman had married and become a householder on his own account during my absence in Australia. Alice knew his address, and gave me the number of his house, which was on Church Street. A few minutes' rapid walking brought me to his door. I had no great expectation of finding him at home, as I deemed it probable he had not returned from wherever he had been going when I met him; but I should be able to find out when he was expected, and would either wait or go in search of him. Fortune favored me for once, however; he had returned more than an hour before. I was ushered into the drawing-room, where I found him playing cribbage with his wife.

"Why, Willie," he exclaimed, advancing to welcome me, "this is kinder than I expected. I hardly looked for you before to-morrow. All the better; we have just been speaking of you. Ellen, this is my old friend, Willie Furlong, the returned convict, whose banishment you have so often heard me deplore."

After exchanging brief courtesies with Mrs. Gray, I turned to her husband.

"Johnny, did you notice anything remarkable about the old gentleman who was with me when we met on Young Street this evening?"

"Old gentleman! who? There was no one with you when I met you."

"Think again, He and I were walking arm in arm, and you had passed us before you recognized me, and mentioned my name."

He looked hard in my face for a moment, and then said positively:

"You are wrong, Willie. You were certainly alone when we met. You were walking slowly, and I must have noticed if any one had been with you."

"It is you who are wrong," I retorted, almost sternly. "I was accompanied by an elderly gentleman, who wore a great coat with fur collar and cuffs, and we were conversing earnestly together when you passed us."

He hesitated an instant, and seemed to consider, but there was no shade of doubt on his face.

"Have it your own way, old boy," he said. "All I can say is, that I saw no one but yourself, and neither did Charley Leitch, who was with me. After parting from you we commented upon your evident abstraction, and the sombre expression of your countenance, which we attributed to your having only recently heard of the sudden death of your Uncle Richard. If any old gentleman had been with you we could not possibly have failed to notice him."

Without a single word by way of explanation or apology, I jumped from my seat, passed out into the hall, seized my hat, and left the house.

III.

Out into the street I rushed like a madman, banging the door after me. I knew that Johnny would follow me for an explanation, so I ran like lightning round the next corner, and thence down to Yonge Street. Then I dropped into a walk, regained my breath, and asked myself what I should do next.

Suddenly I bethought me of Dr. Marsden, an old friend of my uncle's. I hailed a passing cab, and drove to his house. The doctor was in his consultation-room, and alone.

Of course he was surprised to see me, and gave expression to some appropriate words of sympathy at my bereavement. "But how is it that I see you so soon?" he asked--"I understood that you were not expected for some months to come."

Then I began my story, which I related with great circumstantiality of detail, bringing it down to the moment of my arrival at his house. He listened with the closest attention, never interrupting me by a single exclamation until I had finished. Then he began to ask questions, some of which I thought strangely irrelevant.

"Have you enjoyed your usual good health during your residence abroad?"

"Never better in my life. I have not had a moment's illness since you last saw me."

"And how have you prospered in your business enterprises?"

"Reasonably well; but pray doctor, let us confine ourselves to the matter in hand. I have come for friendly, not professional, advice."

"All in good time, my boy," he calmly remarked. This was tantalizing. My strange narrative did not seem to have disturbed his serenity in the least degree.

"Did you have a pleasant passage?" he asked, after a brief pause. "The ocean, I believe, is generally rough at this time of year."

"I felt a little squeamish for a day or two after leaving Melbourne," I replied, "but I soon got over it, and it was not very bad even while it lasted. I am a tolerably good sailor."

"And you have had no special ground of anxiety of late? At least not until you received this wonderful letter"--he added, with a perceptible contraction of his lips, as though trying to repress a smile.

Then I saw what he was driving at.

"Doctor," I exclaimed, with some exasperation in my tone--"pray dismiss from your mind the idea that what I have told you is the result of diseased imagination. I am as sane as you are. The letter itself affords sufficient evidence that I am not quite such a fool as you take me for."

"My dear boy, I don't take you for a fool at all, although you are a little excited just at present. But I thought you said you returned the letter to--ahem--your uncle."

For a moment I had forgotten that important fact. But I was not altogether without evidence that I had not been the victim of a disordered brain. My friend Gridley could corroborate the receipt of the letter and its contents. My cousin could bear witness that I had displayed an acquaintance with facts which I would not have been likely to learn from any one but my uncle. I had referred to his wig and overcoat, and had mentioned to her the name of Mr. Marcus Weatherley--a name which I had never heard before in my life. I called Dr. Marsden's attention to these matters, and asked him to explain them if he could.

"I admit," said the doctor, "that I don't quite see my way to a satisfactory explanation just at present. But let us look the matter squarely in the face. During an acquaintance of nearly thirty years, I always found your uncle a truthful man, who was cautious enough to make no statements about his neighbours that he was not able to prove. Your informant, on the other hand, does not seem to have confined himself to facts. He made a charge of forgery against a gentleman whose moral and commercial integrity are unquestioned by all who know him. I know Marcus Weatherley pretty well, and am not disposed to pronounce him a forger and a scoundrel upon the unsupported evidence of a shadowy old gentleman who appears and disappears in the most mysterious manner, and who cannot be laid hold of and held responsible for his slanders in a court of law. And it is not true, as far as I know and believe, that Marcus Weatherley is embarrassed in his circumstances. Such confidence have I in his solvency and integrity that I would not be afraid to take up all his outstanding paper without asking a question. If you will make inquiry, you will find that my opinion is shared by all the bankers in the city. And I have no hesitation in saying that you will find no acceptances with your uncle's name to them, either in this market or elsewhere."

"That I will try to ascertain to-morrow," I replied. "Meanwhile, Dr. Marsden, will you oblige your old friend's nephew by writing to Mr. Junius Gridley, and asking him to acquaint you with the contents of the letter, and the circumstances under which I received it?"

"It seems an absurd thing to do," he said, "but I will if you like. What shall I say?" and he sat down at his desk to write the letter.

It was written in less than five minutes. It simply asked for the desired information, and requested an immediate reply. Below the doctor's signature I added a short postscript in these words:--

"My story about the letter and its contents is discredited. Pray answer fully, and at once.--W. F. F."

At my request the doctor accompanied me to the Post-office, on Toronto Street, and dropped the letter into the box with his own hands. I bade him good night, and repaired to the Rossin House. I did not feel like encountering Alice again until I could place myself in a more satisfactory light before her. I despatched a messenger to her with a short note stating that I had not discovered anything important, and requesting her not to wait up for me. Then I engaged a room and went to bed.

But not to sleep. All night long I tossed about from one side of the bed to the other; and at daylight, feverish and unrefreshed, I strolled out. I returned in time for breakfast, but ate little or nothing. I longed for the arrival of ten o'clock, when the banks would open.

After breakfast I sat down in the reading-room of the hotel, and vainly tried to fix my attention upon the local columns of the morning's paper. I remember reading over several items time after time, without any comprehension of their meaning. After that I remember--nothing.

Nothing? All was blank for more than five weeks. When consciousness came back to me I found myself in bed in my own old room, in the house on Gerrard Street, and Alice and Dr. Marsden were standing by my bedside.

No need to tell how my hair had been removed, nor about the bags of ice that had been applied to my head. No need to linger over any details of the "pitiless fever that burned in my brain." No need, either, to linger over my progress back to convalescence, and thence to complete recovery. In a week from the time I have mentioned, I was permitted to sit up in bed, propped up by a mountain of pillows. My impatience would brook no further delay, and I was allowed to ask questions about what had happened in the interval which had elapsed since my over wrought nerves gave way under the prolonged strain upon them. First, Junius Gridley's letter in reply to Dr. Marsden was placed in my hands. I have it still in my possession, and I transcribe the following copy from the original now lying before me:--

"BOSTON, Dec. 22nd, 1861.

"DR. MARSDEN:

"In reply to your letter, which has just been received, I have to say that Mr. Furlong and myself became acquainted for the first time during our recent passage from Liverpool to Boston, in the *Persia*, which arrived here Monday last. Mr. Furlong accompanied me home, and remained until Tuesday morning, when I took him to see the Public Library, the State House, the Athenaeum, Faneuil Hall, and other points of interest. We casually dropped into the post-office, and he remarked upon the great number of letters there. At my instigation--made, of course, in jest--he applied at the General Delivery for letters for himself. He received one bearing the Toronto post-mark. He was naturally very much surprised at receiving it, and was not less so at its contents. After reading it he handed it to me, and I also read it carefully. I cannot recollect it word for word, but it professed to come from 'his affectionate uncle, Richard Yardington.' It expressed pleasure at his coming home sooner than had been anticipated, and hinted in rather vague terms at some calamity. He referred to a lady called Alice, and stated that she had not been informed of Mr. Furlong's intended arrival. There was something too, about his presence at home being a recompense to her for recent grief which she had sustained. It also expressed the writer's intention to meet his nephew at the Toronto railway station upon his arrival, and stated that no telegram need be sent. This, as nearly as I can remember, was about all there was in the letter. Mr. Furlong professed to recognise the handwriting as his uncle's. It was a cramped hand, not easy to read, and the signature was so peculiarly formed that I was hardly able to decipher it. The peculiarity consisted of the extreme irregularity in the formation of the letters, no two of which were of equal size; and capitals were interspersed promiscuously, more especially throughout the surname.

"Mr. Furlong was much agitated by the contents of the letter, and was anxious for the arrival of the time of his departure. He left by the B. & A. train at 11.30. This is really all I know about the matter, and I have been anxiously expecting to hear from him ever since he left. I confess that I feel curious, and should be glad to hear from him--that is, of course, unless something is involved which it would be impertinent for a comparative stranger to pry into.

"Yours, &c.,   "JUNIUS H. GRIDLEY."

So that my friend has completely corroborated my account, so far as the letter was concerned. My account, however, stood in no need of corroboration, as will presently appear.

When I was stricken down, Alice and Dr. Marsden were the only persons to whom I had communicated what my uncle had said to me during our walk from the station. They both maintained silence in the matter, except to each other. Between themselves, in the early days of my illness, they discussed it with a good deal of feeling on each side. Alice implicitly believed my story from first to last. She was wise enough to see that I had been made acquainted with matters that I could not possibly have learned through any ordinary channels of communication. In short, she was not so enamoured of professional jargon as to have lost her common sense. The doctor, however, with the mole-blindness of many of his tribe, refused to believe. Nothing of this kind had previously come within the range of his own experience, and it was therefore impossible. He accounted for it all upon the hypothesis of my impending fever. He is not the only physician who mistakes cause for effect, and *vice versa*.

During the second week of my prostration, Mr. Marcus Weatherley absconded.

This event so totally unlooked for by those who had had dealings with him, at once brought his financial condition to light. It was found that he had been really insolvent for several months past. The day after his departure a number of his acceptances became due. These acceptances proved to be four in number, amounting to exactly forty-two thousand dollars. So that that part of my uncle's story was confirmed. One of the acceptances was payable in Montreal, and was for $2,283.76. The other three were payable at different banks in Toronto. These last had been drawn at sixty days, and each of them bore a signature presumed to be that of Richard Yardington. One of them was for $8,972.11; another was for $10,114.63; and the third and last was for $20,629.50. A short sum in simple addition will show us the aggregate of these three amounts--

```
$ 8,972.11
 10,114.63
 20,629.50
 ---------
$39,716.24
```

which was the amount for which my uncle claimed that his name had been forged.

Within a week after these things came to light a letter addressed to the manager of one of the leading banking institutions of Toronto arrived from Mr. Marcus Weatherley. He wrote from New York, but stated that he should leave there within an hour from the time of posting his letter. He voluntarily admitted having forged the name of my uncle to the three acceptances above referred to and entered into other details about his affairs, which, though interesting enough to his creditors at that time, would have no special interest to the public at the present day. The banks where the acceptances had been discounted were wise after the fact, and detected numerous little details wherein the forged signatures differed from the genuine signatures of my Uncle Richard. In each case they pocketed the loss and held their tongues, and I dare say they will not thank me for calling attention to the matter, even at this distance of time.

There is not much more to tell. Marcus Weatherley, the forger, met his fate within a few days after writing his letter from New York. He took passage at New Bedford, Massachusetts, in a sailing vessel called the *Petrel* bound for Havana. The *Petrel* sailed from port on the 12th of January, 1862, and went down in mid-ocean with all hands on the 23rd of the same month. She sank in full sight of the captain and crew of the *City of Baltimore* (Inman Line), but the hurricane prevailing was such that the latter were unable to render any assistance, or to save one of the ill-fated crew from the fury of the waves.

At an early stage in the story I mentioned that the only fictitious element should be the name of one of the characters introduced. The name is that of Marcus Weatherley himself. The person whom I have so designated really bore a different name--one that is still remembered by scores of people in Toronto. He has paid the penalty of his misdeeds, and I see nothing to be gained by perpetuating them in connection with his own proper name. In all other particulars the foregoing narrative is as true as a tolerably retentive memory has enabled me to record it.

I don't propose to attempt any psychological explanation of the events here recorded, for the very sufficient reason that only one explanation is possible. The weird letter and its contents, as has been seen, do not rest upon my testimony alone. With respect to my walk from the station with Uncle Richard, and the communication made by him to me, all the details are as real to my mind as any other incidents of my life. The only obvious deduction is, that I was made the recipient of a communication of the kind which the world is accustomed to regard as supernatural.

Mr. Owen's publishers have my full permission to appropriate this story in the next edition of his "Debatable Land between this World and the Next." Should they do so, their readers will doubtless be favoured with an elaborate analysis of the facts, and with a pseudo-philosophic theory about spiritual communion with human beings. My wife, who is an enthusiastic student of electro-biology, is disposed to believe that Weatherley's mind, overweighted by the knowledge of his forgery, was in some occult manner, and unconsciously to himself, constrained to act upon my own senses. I prefer, however, simply to narrate the facts. I may or may not have my own theory about those facts. The reader is at perfect liberty to form one of his own if he so pleases. I may mention that Dr. Marsden professes to believe to the present day that my mind was disordered by the approach of the fever which eventually struck me down, and that all I have described was merely the result of what he, with delightful periphrasis, calls "an abnormal condition of the system, induced by causes too remote for specific diagnosis."

It will be observed that, whether I was under an hallucination or not, the information supposed to be derived from my uncle was strictly accurate in all its details. The fact that the disclosure subsequently became unnecessary through the confession of Weatherley does not seem to me to afford any argument for the hallucination theory. My uncle's communication was important at the time when it was given to me; and we have no reason for believing that "those who are gone before" are universally gifted with a knowledge of the future.

It was open to me to make the facts public as soon as they became known to me, and had I done so, Marcus Weatherley might have been arrested and punished for his crime. Had not my illness supervened, I think I should have made discoveries in the course of the day following my arrival in Toronto which would have led to his arrest.

Such speculations are profitless enough, but they have often formed the topic of discussion between my wife and myself. Gridley, too, whenever he pays us a visit, invariably revives the subject, which he long ago christened "The Gerrard Street Mystery," although it might just as correctly be called "The Yonge Street Mystery," or, "The Mystery of the Union Station." He has urged me a hundred times over to publish the story; and now, after all these years, I follow his counsel, and adopt his nomenclature in the title.

GAGTOOTH'S IMAGE.

About three o'clock in the afternoon of Wednesday, the fourth of September, 1884, I was riding up Yonge Street, in the city of Toronto, on the top of a crowded omnibus. The omnibus was bound for Thornhill, and my own destination was the intermediate village of Willowdale. Having been in Canada only a short time, and being almost a stranger in Toronto, I dare say I was looking around me with more attention and curiosity than persons who are "native here, and to the manner born," are accustomed to exhibit. We had just passed Isabella Street, and were rapidly nearing Charles Street, when I noticed on my right hand a large, dilapidated frame building, standing in solitary isolation a few feet back from the highway, and presenting the appearance of a veritable Old Curiosity Shop.

A business was carried on here in second hand furniture of the poorest description, and the object of the proprietor seemed to have been to collect about him all sorts of worn-out commodities, and objects which were utterly unmarketable. Everybody who lived in Toronto at the time indicated will remember the establishment, which, as I subsequently learned, was owned and carried on by a man named Robert Southworth, familiarly known to his customers as "Old Bob." I had no sooner arrived abreast of the gateway leading into the yard immediately adjoining the building to the southward, than my eyes rested upon something which instantly caused them to open themselves to their very widest capacity, and constrained me to signal the driver to stop; which he had no sooner done than I alighted from my seat and requested him to proceed on his journey without me. The driver eyed me suspiciously, and evidently regarded me as an odd customer, but he obeyed my request, and drove on northward, leaving me standing in the middle of the street.

From my elevated seat on the roof of the 'bus, I had caught a hurried glimpse of a commonplace-looking little marble figure, placed on the top of a pedestal, in the yard already referred to, where several other figures in marble, wood, bronze, stucco and what not, were exposed for sale.

The particular figure which had attracted my attention was about fifteen inches in height, and represented a little child in the attitude of prayer. Anyone seeing it for the first time would probably have taken it for a representation of the Infant Samuel. I have called it commonplace; and considered as a work of art, such it undoubtedly was; yet it must have possessed a certain distinctive individuality, for the brief glance which I had caught of it, even at that distance, had been sufficient to convince me that the figure was an old acquaintance of mine. It was in consequence of that conviction that I had dismounted from the omnibus, forgetful, for the moment, of everything but the matter which was uppermost in my mind.

I lost no time in passing through the gateway leading into the yard, and in walking up to the pedestal upon which the little figure was placed. Taking the latter in my hand, I found, as I had expected, that it was not attached to the pedestal, which was of totally different material, and much more elaborate workmanship. Turning the figure upside down, my eyes rested on these words, deeply cut into the little circular throne upon which the figure rested:--JACKSON: PEORIA, 1854.

At this juncture the proprietor of the establishment walked up to where I was standing beside the pedestal. "Like to look at something in that way, sir?" he asked--"we have more inside."

"What is the price of this?" I asked, indicating the figure in my hand.

"That, sir; you may have that for fifty cents--of course without the pedestal, which don't belong to it."

"Have you had it on hand long?"

"I don't know, but if you'll step inside for a moment I can tell you. This way, sir."

Taking the figure under my arm, I followed him into what he called "the office"--a small and dirty room, crowded with old furniture in the last stage of dilapidation. From a desk in one corner he took a large tome labelled "Stock Book," to which he referred, after glancing at a hieroglyphical device pasted on the figure which I held under my arm.

"Yes, sir--had that ever since the 14th of March, 1880--bought it at Morris & Blackwell's sale, sir."

"Who and what are Messrs. Morris & Blackwell?" I enquired.

"They *were* auctioneers, down on Adelaide Street, in the city, sir. Failed sometime last winter. Mr. Morris has since died, and I believe Blackwell, the other partner went to the States."

After a few more questions, finding that he knew nothing whatever about the matter beyond what he had already told me, I paid over the fifty cents; and, declining with thanks his offer to send my purchase home to me, I marched off with it down the street, and made the best of my way back to the Rossin House, where I had been staying for some days before.

From what has been said, it will be inferred that I--a stranger in Canada--must have had some special reason for incumbering myself in my travels with an intrinsically worthless piece of common Columbia marble.

I *had* a reason. I had often seen that little figure before; and the last time I had seen it, previous to the occasion above mentioned, had been at the town of Peoria, in the State of Illinois, sometime in the month of June, 1855.

There is a story connected with that little praying figure; a story, which, to me, is a very touching one; and I believe myself to be the only human being capable of telling it. Indeed, *I* am only able to tell a part of it. How the figure came to be sold by auction, in the city of Toronto, at Messrs. Morris & Blackwell's sale on the 14th of March, 1880, or how it ever came to be in this part of the world at all, I know no more than the reader does; but I can probably tell all that is worth knowing about the matter.

In the year 1850, and for I know not how long previously, there lived at Peoria, Illinois, a journeyman-blacksmith named Abner Fink. I mention the date, 1850, because it was in that year that I myself settled in Peoria, and first had any knowledge of him; but I believe he had then been living there for some length of time. He was employed at the foundry of Messrs. Gowanlock and Van Duzer, and was known for an excellent workman, of steady habits, and good moral character-- qualifications which were by no means universal, nor even common, among persons of his calling and degree of life, at the time and place of which I am writing. But he was still more conspicuous (on the *lucus a non lucendo* principle) for another quality--that of reticence. It was very rarely indeed that he spoke to anyone, except when called upon to reply to a question; and even then it was noticeable that he invariably employed the fewest and most concise words in his vocabulary. If brevity were the body, as well as the soul of wit, Fink must have been about the wittiest man that ever lived, the Monosyllabic Traveller not excepted. He never received a letter from any one during the whole time of his stay at Peoria; nor, so far as was known, did he ever write to any one. Indeed, there was no evidence that he was able to write. He never went to church, nor even to "meeting;" never attended any public entertainment; never took any holidays. All his time was spent either at the foundry where he worked, or at the boarding-house where he lodged. In the latter place, the greater part of his hours of relaxation were spent in looking either out of the window or into the fire; thinking, apparently, about nothing particular. All endeavours on the part of his fellow boarders to draw him into conversation were utterly fruitless. No one in the place knew anything about his past life, and when his fellow-journeymen in the workshop attempted to inveigle him into any confidence on that subject, he had a trick of calling up a harsh and sinister expression of countenance which effectually nipped all such experiments in the bud. Even his employers failed to elicit anything from him on this head, beyond the somewhat vague piece of intelligence that he hailed from "down east." The foreman of the establishment with a desperate attempt at facetiousness, used to say of him, that no one knew who he was, where he came from, where he was going to, or what he was going to do when he got there.

And yet, this utter lack of sociability could scarcely have arisen from positive surliness or unkindness of disposition. Instances were not wanting in which he had given pretty strong evidence that he carried beneath that rugged and uncouth exterior a kinder and more gentle heart than is possessed by most men. Upon one occasion he had jumped at the imminent peril of his life, from the bridge which spans the Illinois river just above the entrance to the lake, and had fished up a drowning child from its depths and borne it to the shore in safety. In doing so he had been compelled to swim through a swift and strong current which would have swamped any swimmer with one particle less strength, endurance and pluck. At another time, hearing his landlady say, at dinner, that an execution was in the house of a sick man with a large family, at the other end of the town, he left his dinner untouched, trudged off to the place indicated, and--though the debtor was an utter stranger to him--paid off the debt and costs in full, without taking any assignment of the judgment or other security. Then he went quietly back to his work. From my knowledge of the worthless and impecunious character of the debtor, I am of opinion that Fink never received a cent in the way of reimbursement.

In personal appearance he was short and stout. His age, when I first knew him, must have been somewhere in the neighbourhood of thirty-five. The only peculiarity about his face was an abnormal formation of one of his front teeth, which protruded, and stuck out almost horizontally. This, as may be supposed, did not tend to improve an expression of countenance which in other respects was not very prepossessing. One of the anvil-strikers happening to allude to him one day in his absence by the name of "Gagtooth," the felicity of the sobriquet at once commended itself to the good taste of the other hands in the shop, who thereafter commonly spoke of him by that name, and eventually it came to be applied to him by every one in the town.

My acquaintance with him began when I had been in Peoria about a week. I may premise that I am a physician and surgeon--a graduate of Harvard. Peoria was at that time a comparatively new place, but it gave promise of going ahead rapidly;

a promise, by the way, which it has since amply redeemed. Messrs. Gowanlock and Van Duzer's foundry was a pretty extensive one for a small town in a comparatively new district. They kept about a hundred and fifty hands employed all the year round, and during the busy season this number was more than doubled. It was in consequence of my having received the appointment of medical attendant to that establishment that I buried myself in the west, instead of settling down in my native State of Massachusetts.

Poor Gagtooth was one of my first surgical patients. It came about in this wise. At the foundry, two days in the week, viz., Tuesdays and Fridays, were chiefly devoted to what is called "casting." On these days it was necessary to convey large masses of melted iron, in vessels specially manufactured for that purpose, from one end of the moulding shop to the other. It was, of course, very desirable that the metal should not be allowed to cool while in transit, and that as little time as possible should be lost in transferring it from the furnace to the moulds. For this purpose Gagtooth's services were frequently called into requisition, as he was by far the strongest man about the place, and could without assistance carry one end of one of the vessels, which was considered pretty good work for two ordinary men.

Well, one unlucky Friday afternoon he was hard at work at this employment, and as was usual with all the hands in the moulding shop at such times, he was stripped naked from the waist upwards. He was gallantly supporting one end of one of the large receptacles already mentioned, which happened to be rather fuller than usual of the red-hot molten metal. He had nearly reached the moulding-box into which the contents of the vessel were to be poured, when he stumbled against a piece of scantling which was lying in his way. He fell, and as a necessary consequence his end of the vessel fell likewise, spilling the contents all over his body, which was literally deluged by the red, hissing, boiling liquid fire. It must have seemed to the terror-stricken onlookers like a bath of blood.

Further details of the frightful accident, and of my treatment of the case, might be interesting to such of the readers of this book as happen to belong to my own profession; but to general readers such details would be simply shocking. How even his tremendous vitality and vigour of constitution brought him through it all is a mystery to me to this day. I am thirty-six years older than I was at that time. Since then I have acted as surgeon to a fighting regiment all through the great rebellion.

I have had patients of all sorts of temperaments and constitutions under my charge, but never have I been brought into contact with a case which seemed more hopeless in my eyes. He must surely have had more than one life in him. I have never had my hands on so magnificent a specimen of the human frame as his was; and better still--and this doubtless contributed materially to his recovery--I have never had a case under my management where the patient bore his sufferings with such uniform fortitude and endurance. Suffice it to say that he recovered, and that his face bore no traces of the frightful ordeal through which he had passed. I don't think he was ever quite the same man as before his accident. I think his nervous system received a shock which eventually tended to shorten his life. But he was still known as incomparably the strongest man in Peoria, and continued to perform the work of two men at the moulding-shop on casting days. In every other respect he was apparently the same; not a whit more disposed to be companionable than before his accident. I used frequently to meet him on the street, as he was going to and fro between his boarding-house and the work-shop. He was always alone, and more than once I came to a full stop and enquired after his health, or anything else that seemed to afford a feasible topic for conversation. He was uniformly civil, and even respectful, but confined his remarks to replying to my questions, which, as usual, was done in the fewest words.

During the twelve months succeeding his recovery, so far as I am aware, nothing occurred worthy of being recorded in Gagtooth's annals. About the expiration of that time, however, his landlady, by his authority, at his request, and in his presence, made an announcement to the boarders assembled at the dinner-table which, I should think, must literally have taken away their breaths.

Gagtooth was going to be married!

I don't suppose it would have occasioned greater astonishment if it had been announced as an actual fact that The Illinois river had commenced to flow backwards. It was surprising, incredible, but, like many other surprising and incredible things, it was true. Gagtooth was really and truly about to marry. The object of his choice was his landlady's sister, by name Lucinda Bowlsby. How or when the wooing had been carried on, how the engagement had been led up to, and in what terms the all-important question had been propounded, I am not prepared to say. I need hardly observe that none of the boarders had entertained the faintest suspicion that anything of the kind was impending. The courtship, from first to last, must have been somewhat of a piece with that of the late Mr. Barkis. But alas! Gagtooth did not settle his affections so judiciously, nor did he draw such a prize in the matrimonial lottery as Barkis did. Two women more entirely dissimilar, in every respect, than Peggotty and Lucinda Bowlsby can hardly be imagined. Lucinda was nineteen years of age. She was pretty, and, for a girl of her class and station in life, tolerably well educated. But she was notwithstanding a light, giddy creature--and, I fear, something worse, at that time. At all events, she had a very questionable sort of reputation among the boarders in the house, and was regarded with suspicion by everyone who knew anything about her poor Gagtooth alone excepted.

In due time the wedding took place. It was solemnized at the boarding-house; and the bride and bridegroom disdaining to defer to the common usage, spent their honeymoon in their own house. Gagtooth had rented and furnished a little frame dwelling on the outskirts of the town, on the bank of the river; and thither the couple retired as soon as the hymeneal knot was tied. Next morning the bridegroom made his appearance at his forge and went to work as usual, as though nothing had occurred to disturb the serenity of his life.

Time passed by. Rumours now and then reached my ears to the effect that Mrs. Fink was not behaving herself very well, and that she was leading her husband rather a hard life of it. She had been seen driving out into the country with a young lawyer from Springfield, who occasionally came over to Peoria to attend the sittings of the District Court. She moreover had the reputation of habitually indulging in the contents of the cup that cheers and likewise inebriates. However, in the regular course of things, I was called upon to assist at the first appearance upon life's stage of a little boy, upon whom his parents bestowed the name of Charlie.

The night of Charlie's birth was the first time I had ever been in the house, and if I remember aright it was the first time I had ever set eyes on Mrs. Fink since her marriage. I was not long in making up my mind about her; and I had ample opportunity for forming an opinion as to her character, for she was unable to leave her bed for more than a month, during which time I was in attendance upon her almost daily. I also attended little Charlie through measels, scarlet-rash, whooping-cough, and all his childish ailments; and in fact I was a pretty regular visitor at the house from the time of his birth until his father left the neighbourhood, as I shall presently have to relate. I believe Mrs. Fink to have been not merely a profligate woman, but a thoroughly bad and heartless one in every respect. She was perfectly indifferent to her husband, whom she shamefully neglected, and almost indifferent to her child. She seemed to care for nothing in the world but dress and strong waters; and to procure these there was no depth of degradation to which she would not stoop.

As a result of my constant professional attendance upon his mother during the first month of little Charlie's life, I became better acquainted with his father than anyone in Peoria had ever done. He seemed to know that I saw into and sympathized with his domestic troubles, and my silent sympathy seemed to afford him some consolation. As the months and years passed by, his wife's conduct became worse and worse, and his affections centered themselves entirely upon his child, whom he loved with a passionate affection to which I have never seen a parallel.

And Charlie was a child made to be loved. When he was two years old he was beyond all comparison the dearest and most beautiful little fellow I have ever seen. His fat, plump, chubby little figure, modelled after Cupid's own; his curly flaxen hair; his matchless complexion, fair and clear as the sky on a sunny summer day; and his bright, round, expressive eyes, which imparted intelligence to his every feature, combined to make him the idol of his father, the envy of all the mothers in town, and the admiration of every one who saw him. At noon, when the great foundry-bell rang, which was the signal for the workmen to go to dinner Charlie might regularly be seen, toddling as fast as his stout little legs could spin, along the footpath leading over the common in the direction of the workshops. When about halfway across, he would be certain to meet his father, who, taking the child up in his bare, brawny, smoke-begrimed arms, would carry him home--the contrast between the two strongly suggesting Vulcan and Cupid. At six o'clock in the evening, when the bell announced that work was over for the day, a similar little drama was enacted. It would be difficult to say whether Vulcan or Cupid derived the greater amount of pleasure from these semi-daily incidents. After tea, the two were never separate for a moment. While the mother was perhaps busily engaged in the perusal of some worthless novel, the father would sit with his darling on his knee, listening to his childish prattle, and perhaps so far going out of himself as to tell the child a little story. It seemed to be an understood thing that the mother should take no care or notice of the boy during her husband's presence in the house. Regularly, when the clock on the chimney-piece struck eight, Charlie would jump down from his father's knee and run across the room for his night-dress, returning to his father to have it put on. When this had been done he would kneel down and repeat a simple little prayer, in which One who loved little children like Charlie was invoked to bless father and mother and make him a good boy; after which his father would place him in his little crib, where he soon slept the sleep of happy childhood.

My own house was not far from theirs, and I was so fond of Charlie that it was no uncommon thing for me to drop in upon them for a few minutes, when returning from my office in the evening. Upon one occasion I noticed the child more particularly than usual while he was in the act of saying his prayers. His eyes were closed, his plump little hands were clasped, and his cherubic little face was turned upwards with an expression of infantile trustfulness and adoration which I shall never forget. I have never seen, nor do I ever expect to see, anything else half so beautiful. When he arose from his knees and came up to me to say "Good Night," I kissed his upturned little face with even greater fervour than usual. After he had been put to bed I mentioned the matter to his father, and said something about my regret that the child's expression had not been caught by a sculptor and fixed in stone.

I had little idea of the effect my remarks were destined to produce. A few evenings afterwards he informed me, much to my surprise, that he had determined to act upon the idea which my words had suggested to his mind, and that he had instructed Heber Jackson, the marble-cutter, to go to work at a "stone likeness" of little Charlie, and to finish it up as soon as possible. He did not seem to understand that the proper performance of such a task required anything more than mere mechanical skill, and that an ordinary tomb-stone cutter was scarcely the sort of artist to do justice to it.

However, when the "stone-likeness" was finished and sent home, I confess I was astonished to see how well Jackson had succeeded. He had not, of course, caught the child's exact expression. It is probable, indeed, that he never saw the expression on Charlie's face, which had seemed so beautiful to me, and which had suggested to me the idea of its being "embodied in marble," as the professionals call it. But the image was at all events, according to order, a "likeness." The true lineaments were there and I would have recognised it for a representation of my little friend at the first glance, wherever I might have seen it. In short, it was precisely one of those works of art which have no artistic value whatever for any one who is unacquainted with, or uninterested in, the subject represented; but knowing and loving little Charlie as I did, I confess that I used to contemplate Jackson's piece of workmanship with an admiration and enthusiasm which the contents of Italian galleries have failed to arouse in me.

Well, the months flew by until some time in the spring of 1855, when the town was electrified by the sudden and totally unexpected failure of Messrs. Gowanlock and Van Duzer, who up to that time were currently reported to be one of the wealthiest and most thriving firms in the State. Their failure was not only a great misfortune for the workmen, who were thus thrown out of present employment--for the creditors did not carry on the business--but was regarded as a public calamity to the town and neighbourhood, the prosperity whereof had been enhanced in no inconsiderable degree by the carrying on of so extensive an establishment in their midst, and by the enterprise and energy of the proprietors, both of whom were first-rate business men. The failure was in no measure attributed either to dishonesty or want of prudence on the part of Messrs. Gowanlock and Van Duzer, but simply to the invention of a new patent which rendered valueless the particular agricultural implement which constituted the specialty of the establishment, and of which there was an enormous stock on hand. There was not the shadow of a hope of the firm being able to get upon its legs again. The partners surrendered everything almost to the last dollar, and shortly afterwards left Illinois for California.

Now, this failure, which more or less affected the entire population of Peoria, was especially disastrous to poor Fink. For past years he had been saving money, and as Messrs. Gowanlock and Van Duzer allowed interest at a liberal rate upon all deposits left in their hands by their workmen, all his surplus earnings remained untouched. The consequence was that the accumulations of years were swamped at one fell swoop, and he found himself reduced to poverty. And as though misfortune was not satisfied with visiting him thus heavily, the very day of the failure he was stricken down by typhoid fever: not the typhoid fever known in Canada--which is bad enough--but the terrible putrid typhoid of the west, which is known nowhere else on the face of the globe, and in which the mortality in some years reaches forty per cent.

Of course I was at once called in. I did my best for the patient, which was very little. I tried hard, however, to keep his wife sober, and to compel her to nurse him judiciously. As for little Charlie, I took him home with me to my own house, where he remained until his father was so far convalescent as to prevent all fear of infection. Meanwhile I knew nothing about Gagtooth's money having been deposited in the hands of his employers, and consequently was ignorant of his loss. I did not learn this circumstance for weeks afterwards, and of course had no reason for supposing that his wife was in anywise straitened for money. Once, when her husband had been prostrated for about a fortnight, I saw her with a roll of bank notes in her hand. Little did I suspect how they had been obtained.

Shortly after my patient had begun to sit up in his arm-chair for a little while every day, he begged so hard for little Charlie's presence that, as soon as I was satisfied that all danger of infection was past, I consented to allow the child to return to his own home. In less than a month afterwards the invalid was able to walk out in the garden for a few minutes every day when the weather was favourable, and in these walks Charlie was his constant companion. The affection of the poor fellow for his flaxen-haired darling was manifested in every glance of his eye, and in every tone of his voice. He would kiss the little chap and pat him on the head a hundred times a day. He would tell him stories until he himself was completely exhausted; and although I knew that this tended to retard his complete recovery, I had not the heart to forbid it. I have often since felt thankful that I never made any attempt to do so.

At last the fifteenth of September arrived. On the morning of that day Messrs. Rockwell and Dunbar's Combined Circus and Menagerie made a triumphal entry into Peoria, and was to exhibit on the green, down by the river bank. The performance had been ostentatiously advertised and placarded on every dead wall in town for a month back, and all the children in the place, little Charlie included, were wild on the subject. Signor Martigny was to enter a den containing three full-grown lions, and was to go through the terrific and disgusting ordeal usual on such occasions. Gagtooth, of course, was unable to go; but, being unwilling to deny his child any reasonable pleasure, he had consented to Charlie's going with his mother. I happened to be passing the house on my way homewards to dinner, just as the pair were about to start, and called in to say good-bye to my patient. Never shall I forget the embrace and the kiss which the father bestowed upon the little fellow. I can see them now, after all these years, almost as distinctly as I saw them on that terrible fifteenth of September, 1855. They perfectly clung to each other, and seemed unwilling to part even for the two or three hours during which the performance was to last. I can see the mother too, impatiently waiting in the doorway, and telling Charlie that if he didn't stop that nonsense they would be too late to see Sampson killing the lion. She--Heaven help her!--thought nothing and cared nothing about the pleasure the child was to derive from the entertainment. She was only anxious on her own account; impatient to shew her good looks and her cheap finery to the two thousand and odd people assembled under the huge tent.

At last they started. Gagtooth got up and walked to the door, following them with his eye as far as he could see them down the dusty street. Then he returned and sat down in his chair. Poor fellow! he was destined never to see either of them alive again.

Notwithstanding her fear lest she might not arrive in time for the commencement of the performance, Mrs. Fink and her charge reached the ground at least half an hour before the ticket office was opened; and I regret to say that that half hour was sufficient to enable her to form an acquaintance with one of the property men of the establishment, to whom she contrived to make herself so agreeable that he passed her and Charlie into the tent free of charge. She was not admitted at the front entrance, but from the tiring-room at the back whence the performers enter. She sat down just at the left of this entrance, immediately adjoining the lion's cage. Ere long the performance commenced. Signor Martigny, when his turn came, entered the cage as per announcement; but he was not long in discovering by various signs not to be mistaken that his charges were in no humour to be played with on that day. Even the ring master from his place in the centre of the ring, perceived that old King of the Forest, the largest and most vicious of the lions, was meditating mischief, and called to the Signor to come out of the cage. The Signor, keeping his eye steadily fixed on the brute, began a retrograde movement from the den. He had the door open, and was swiftly backing through, when, with a roar that seemed to shake the very earth, old King sprang upon him from the opposite side of the cage, dashing him to the ground like a ninepin, and rushed through the aperture into the crowd. Quick as lightning the other two followed, and thus three savage lions were loose and unshackled in the midst of upwards of two thousand men, women and children.

I wish to linger over the details as briefly as possible. I am thankful to say that I was not present, and that I am unable to describe the occurrence from personal observation.

Poor little Charlie and his mother, sitting close to the cage, were the very first victims. The child himself, I think, and hope, never knew what hurt him. His skull was fractured by one stroke of the brute's paw. Signor Martigny escaped with his right arm slit into ribbons. Big Joe Pentland, the clown, with one well-directed stroke of a crowbar, smashed Old King of the Forest's jaw into a hundred pieces, but not before it had closed in the left breast of Charlie's mother. She lived for nearly an hour afterwards, but never uttered a syllable. I wonder if she was conscious. I wonder if it was permitted to her to realize what her sin--for sin it must have been, in contemplation, if not in deed--had brought upon herself and her child. Had she paid her way into the circus, and entered in front, instead of coquetting with the property-man, she would have been sitting under a different part of the tent, and neither she nor Charlie would have sustained any injury, for the two younger lions were shot before they had leapt ten paces from the cage door. Old King was easily despatched after Joe Pentland's tremendous blow. Besides Charlie and his mother, two men and one woman were killed on the spot: another woman died next day from the injuries received, and several other persons were more or less severely hurt.

Immediately after dinner I had driven out into the country to pay a professional visit, so that I heard nothing about what had occurred until some hours afterwards. I was informed of it, however, before I reached the town, on my way homeward. To say that I was inexpressibly shocked and grieved would merely be to repeat a very stupid platitude, and to say that I was a human being. I had learned to love poor little Charlie almost as dearly as I loved my own children. And his father--what would be the consequence to him?

I drove direct to his house, which was filled with people--neighbours and others who had called to administer such consolation as the circumstances would admit of. I am not ashamed to confess that the moment my eyes rested upon the bereaved father I burst into tears. He sat with his child's body in his lap, and seemed literally transformed into stone. A breeze came in through the open doorway and stirred his thin iron-gray locks, as he sat there in his arm chair. He was unconscious of everything--even of the presence of strangers. His eyes were fixed and glazed. Not a sound of any kind, not even a moan, passed his lips; and it was only after feeling his pulse that I was able to pronounce with certainty that he was alive. One single gleam of animation overspread his features for an instant when I gently removed the crushed corpse from his knees, and laid it on the bed, but he quickly relapsed into stolidity. I was informed that he had sat thus ever since he had first received the corpse from the arms of Joe Pentland, who had brought it home without changing his clown's dress. Heaven grant that I may never look upon such a sight again as the poor, half-recovered invalid presented during the whole of that night and for several days afterwards.

For the next three days I spent all the time with him I possibly could, for I dreaded either a relapse of the fever or the loss of his reason. The Neighbours were very kind, and took upon themselves the burden of everything connected with the funeral. As for Fink himself, he seemed to take everything for granted, and interfered with nothing. When the time arrived for fastening down the coffin lids, I could not bear to permit that ceremony to be performed without affording him an opportunity of kissing the dead lips of his darling for the last time. I gently led him up to the side of the bed upon which the two coffins were placed. At sight of his little boy's dead face, he fainted, and before he revived I had the lids fastened down. It would have been cruelty to subject him to the ordeal a second time.

The day after the funeral he was sufficiently recovered from the shock to be able to talk. He informed me that he had concluded to leave the neighbourhood, and requested me to draw up a poster, advertising all his furniture and effects for sale by auction. He intended, he said, to sell everything except Charlie's clothes and his own, and these, together with a lock of the child's hair and a few of his toys, were all he intended to take away with him.

"But of course," I remarked, "you don't intend to sell the stone likeness?"

He looked at me rather strangely, and made no reply. I glanced around the room, and, to my surprise, the little statue was nowhere to be seen. It then occurred to me that I had not noticed it since Gagtooth had been taken ill.

"By the by, where is it?" I enquired--"I don't see it."

After a moment's hesitation he told me the whole story. It was then that I learned for the first time that he had lost all his savings through the failure of Messrs. Gowanlock and Van Duzer, and that the morning when he had been taken ill there had been only a dollar in the house. On that morning he had acquainted his wife with his loss, but had strictly enjoined secrecy upon her, as both Gowanlock and Van Duzer had promised him most solemnly that inasmuch as they regarded their indebtedness to him as being upon a different footing from their ordinary liabilities, he should assuredly be paid in full out of the first money at their command. He had implicit reliance upon their word, and requested me to take charge of the money upon its arrival, and to keep it until he instructed me, by post or otherwise, how to dispose of it. To this I, of course, consented. The rest of the story he could only repeat upon the authority of his wife, but I have no reason for disbelieving any portion of it. It seems that a day or two after his illness commenced, and after he had become insensible, his wife had been at her wits' end for money to provide necessaries for the house, and I dare say she spent more for liquor than for necessaries. She declared that she had made up her mind to apply to me for a loan, when a stranger called at the house, attracted, as he said, by the little image, which had been placed in the front window, and was thus visible to passers by. He announced himself as Mr. Silas Pomeroy, merchant, of Myrtle Street, Springfield. He said that the face of the little image strikingly reminded him of the face of a child of his own which had died some time before. He had not supposed that the figure was a likeness of any one, and had stepped in, upon the impulse of the moment, in the hope that he might be able to purchase it. He was willing to pay a liberal price. The negotiation ended in his taking the image away with him, and leaving a hundred dollars in its stead; on which sum Mrs. Fink had kept house ever since. Her husband, of course, knew nothing of this for weeks afterwards. When he began to get better, his wife had acquainted him with the facts. He had found no fault with her, as he had determined to repurchase the image at any cost, so soon as he might be able to earn money enough. As for getting a duplicate, that was out of the question, for Heber Jackson had been carried off by the typhoid epidemic, and Charlie had changed considerably during the fifteen months which had elapsed since the image had been finished. And now poor little Charlie himself was gone, and the great desire of his father's heart was to regain possession of the image. With that view, as soon as the sale should be over he would start for Springfield, tell his story to Pomeroy, and offer him his money back again. As to any further plans, he did not know, he said, what he would do, or where he would go; but he would certainly never live in Peoria again.

In a few days the sale took place, and Gagtooth started for Springfield with about three hundred dollars in his pocket. Springfield is seventy miles from Peoria. He was to return in about ten days, by which time a tombstone was to be ready for Charlie's grave. He had not ordered one for his wife, who was not buried in the same grave with the child, but in one just beside him.

He returned within the ten days. His journey had been a fruitless one. Pomeroy had become insolvent, and had absconded from Springfield a month before. No one knew whither he had gone, but he must have taken the image with him, as it was not among the effects which he had left behind him. His friends knew that he was greatly attached to the image, in consequence of its real or fancied resemblance to his dead child. Nothing more reasonable then than to suppose that he had taken it away with him.

Gagtooth announced to me his determination of starting on an expedition to find Pomeroy, and never giving up the search while his money held out. He had no idea where to look for the fugitive, but rather thought he would try California first. He could hardly expect to receive any remittance from Gowanlock and Van Duzer for some months to come, but he would acquaint me with his address from time to time, and, if anything arrived from them I could forward it to him.

And so, having seen the tombstone set up over little Charlie's grave, he bade me good-bye, and that was the last time I ever saw him, alive.

There is little more to tell. I supposed him to be in the far west, prosecuting his researches, until one night in the early spring of the following year. Charlie and his mother had been interred in a corner of the churchyard adjoining the second Baptist Church, which at that time was on the very outskirts of the town, in a lonely, unfrequented spot, not far from the iron bridge. Late in the evening of the seventh of April, 1856, a woman passing along the road in the cold, dim twilight, saw a bulky object stretched out on Charlie's grave. She called at the nearest house, and stated her belief that a man was lying dead in the churchyard. Upon investigation, her surmise proved to be correct.

And that man was Gagtooth.

Dead; partially no doubt, from cold and exposure; but chiefly, I believe, from a broken heart. Where had he spent the six months which had elapsed since I bade him farewell?

To this question I am unable to reply; but this much was evident: he had dragged himself back just in time to die on the grave of the little boy whom he had loved so dearly, and whose brief existence had probably supplied the one bright spot in his father's life.

I had him buried in the same grave with Charlie; and there, on the banks of the Illinois river, "After life's fitful fever he sleeps well."

I never received any remittance from his former employers, nor did I ever learn anything further of Silas Pomeroy. Indeed, so many years have rolled away since the occurrence of the events above narrated; years pregnant with great events to the American Republic; events, I am proud to say, in which I bore my part: that the wear and tear of life had nearly obliterated all memory of the episode from my mind, until, as detailed in the opening paragraphs of this story, I saw "Gagtooth's Image," from the top of a Thornhill omnibus. That image is now in my possession, and no extremity less urgent than that under which it was sold to Silas Pomeroy, of Myrtle Street, Springfield, will ever induce me to part with it.

THE Haunted House on Duchess Street.

BEING A NARRATION OF CERTAIN STRANGE EVENTS ALLEGED TO HAVE TAKEN PLACE AT YORK, UPPER CANADA, IN OR ABOUT THE YEAR 1823.

"O'er all there hung the Shadow of a Fear;
A sense of mystery the spirit daunted;
And said, as plain as whisper in the ear,
The place is haunted."--HOOD.

I.--OUTSIDE THE HOUSE.

I suppose there are at least a score of persons living in Toronto at the present moment who remember that queer old house on Duchess street. Not that there was anything specially remarkable about the house itself, which indeed, in its best days, presented an aspect of rather snug respectability. But the events I am about to relate invested it with an evil reputation, and made it an object to be contemplated at a safe distance, rather than from any near approach. Youngsters on their way to school were wont to eye it askance as they hurried by on their way to their daily tasks. Even children of a larger growth manifested no unbecoming desire to penetrate too curiously into its inner mysteries, and for years its threshold was seldom or never crossed by anybody except Simon Washburn or some of his clerks, who about once in every twelvemonth made a quiet entry upon the premises and placed in the front windows announcements to the effect that the place was "For Sale or To Let." The printing of these announcements involved a useless expenditure of capital, for, from the time when the character of the house became matter of notoriety, no one could be induced to try the experiment of living in it. In the case of a house, no less than in that of an individual, a bad name is more easily gained than lost, and in the case of the house on Duchess street its uncanny repute clung to it with a persistent grasp which time did nothing to relax. It was distinctly and emphatically a place to keep away from.

The house was originally built by one of the Ridout family--I think by the Surveyor-General himself--soon after the close of the war of 1812, and it remained intact until a year or two after the town of York became the city of Toronto, when it was partly demolished and converted into a more profitable investment. The new structure, which was a shingle or stave factory, was burned down in 1843 or 1844, and the site thenceforward remained unoccupied until comparatively recent times. When I visited the spot a few weeks since I encountered not a little difficulty in fixing upon the exact site, which is covered by an unprepossessing row of dark red brick, presenting the aspect of having stood there from time immemorial, though as I am informed, the houses have been erected within the last quarter of a century. Unattractive as they appear, however, they are the least uninviting feature in the landscape, which is prosaic and squalid beyond description. Rickety, tumble-down tenements of dilapidated lath and plaster stare the beholder in the face at every turn. During the greater part of the day the solitude of the neighbourhood remains unbroken save by the tread of some chance wayfarer like myself, and a general atmosphere of the abomination of desolation reigns supreme. Passing along the un-frequented pavement, one finds it difficult to realize the fact that this was once a not unfashionable quarter of the capital of Upper Canada.

The old house stood forty or fifty feet back from the roadway, on the north side, overlooking the waters of the bay. The lot was divided from the street by a low picket fence, and admission to the enclosure was gained by means of a small gate. In those remote times there were few buildings intervening between Duchess street and the water front, and those few were not very pretentious; so that when the atmosphere was free from fog you could trace from the windows of the upper story the entire hithermost shore of the peninsula which has since become The Island. The structure itself, like most buildings then erected in York, was of frame. It was of considerable dimensions for those days, and must have contained at least eight or nine rooms. It was two stories high, and had a good deal of painted fret-work about the windows of the upper story. A stately elm stood immediately in the rear, and its wide-spreading branches overshadowed the greater part of the back yard and outbuildings. And that is all I have been able to learn about the exterior aspect of the place.

II.--INSIDE THE HOUSE.

A small porch-door, about half way down the western side, furnished the ordinary mode of entrance to and exit from the house. This door opened into an apartment which served the double purpose of sitting-room and dining-room, and which was connected by an inner door with the kitchen and back premises. There was, however, a rather wide-mouthed front entrance, approached by a short flight of wooden steps, and opening into a fair-sized hall. To the right of the hall, as you entered, a door opened into what served as a drawing-room, which was seldom used, as the occupants of the house were not given to receiving much fashionable company. To the left of the hall, another door opened into the dining-room already mentioned. A stairway facing the front entrance, conducted you to the upper story, which consisted of several bed-rooms and a large apartment in front. This latter must have been by long odds the pleasantest room in the house. It was of comfortable dimensions, well lighted, and cheerful as to its outlook. Two front windows commanded a prospect of the bay and the peninsula, while a third window on the eastern side overlooked the valley of the Don, which was by no means the stagnant pool which it was destined to become in later years. The only entrance to this chamber was a door placed directly to the right hand at the head of the stairway, which stairway, it may be mentioned, consisted of exactly seventeen steps. A small bedroom in the rear was accessible only by a separate door at the back of the upper hallway, and was thus not directly connected with the larger apartment.

I am not informed as to the precise number and features of the other rooms in the upper story, except that is they were bedrooms; nor is any further information respecting them essential to a full comprehension of the narrative. Why I have been so precise as to what may at first appear trivial details will hereafter appear.

III.--THE TENANTS OF THE HOUSE.

As already mentioned, the house was probably built by Surveyor-General Ridout;--but it does not appear that either he or any member of his family ever resided there. The earliest occupant of whom I have been able to find any trace was Thomas Mercer Jones--the gentleman, I presume, who was afterwards connected with the Canada Land Company. Whether he was the first tenant I am unable to say, but a gentleman bearing that name dwelt there during the latter part of the year 1816, and appears to have been a well-known citizen of Little York. In 1819 the tenant was a person named McKechnie, as to whom I have been unable to glean any information whatever beyond the bare fact that he was a pewholder in St. James's church. He appears to have given place to one of the numerous members of the Powell family.

But the occupant with whom this narrative is more immediately concerned was a certain ex-military man named Bywater, who woke up the echoes of York society for a few brief months, between sixty and seventy years ago, and who, after passing a lurid interval of his misspent life in this community, solved the great problem of human existence by falling down stairs and breaking his neck. Captain Stephen Bywater was a *mauvais sujet* of the most pronounced stamp. He came of a good family in one of the Midland Counties of England; entered the army at an early age, and was present on a certain memorable Sunday at Waterloo, on which occasion he is said to have borne himself gallantly and well. But he appears to have had a deep vein of ingrained vice in his composition, which perpetually impelled him to crooked paths. Various ugly stories were current about him, for all of which there was doubtless more or less foundation. It was said that he had been caught cheating at play, and that he was an adept in all the rascalities of the turf. The deplorable event which led to the resignation of his commission made considerable noise at the time of its occurrence. A young brother officer whom he had swindled out of large sums of money, was forced by him into a duel, which was fought on the French coast, in the presence of two seconds and a military surgeon. There seems to have been no doubt that the villainous captain fired too soon. At any rate, the youth who had been inveigled into staking his life on the issue was left dead on the field, while the aggressor rode off unscathed, followed by the execrations of his own second. A rigid enquiry was instituted, but the principal witnesses were not forthcoming, and the murderer--for as such he was commonly regarded--escaped the punishment which everybody considered he had justly merited. The severance of his connection with the army was a foregone conclusion, and he was formally expelled from his club. He was socially sent to Coventry, and his native land soon became for him a most undesirable place of abode. Then he crossed the Atlantic and made his way to Upper Canada, where, after a while, he turned up at York, and became the tenant of the house on Duchess street.

At the time of his arrival in this country, which must have been some time in 1822, or perhaps early in 1823, Captain Bywater was apparently about forty years of age. He was a bachelor and possessed of some means. For a very brief period he contrived to make his way into the select society of the Provincial capital; but it soon became known that he was the aristocratic desperado who had so ruthlessly shot down young Remy Errington on the sands near Boulogne, and who had the reputation of being one of the most unmitigated scamps who ever wore uniform. York society in those days could swallow a good deal in a man of good birth and competent fortune, but it could not swallow even a well-to-do bachelor of good family and marriageable age who had been forced to resign his commission, and had been expelled from a not too straight-laced London club, by a unanimous vote of the committee. Captain Bywater was dropped with a suddenness and severity which he could not fail to understand. He received no more invitations from mothers with marriageable daughters, and when he presented himself at their doors informally and forbidden he found nobody at home. Ladies ceased to recognise him on the street, and gentlemen received his bows with a response so frigid that he readily comprehended the state of affairs. He perceived that his day of grace was past, and accepted his fate with a supercilious shrug of his broad shoulders.

But the Captain was a gregarious animal, to whom solitude was insupportable. Society of some sort was a necessity of his existence, and as the company of ladies and gentlemen, was no longer open to him, he sought consolation among persons of a lower grade in the social scale. He began to frequent bar-rooms and other places of public resort, and as he was free with his money he had no difficulty in finding companions of a certain sort who were ready and willing enough to drink at his expense, and to listen to the braggadocio tales of the doughty deeds achieved by him during his campaign in the Peninsula. In a few weeks he found himself the acknowledged head and front of a little coterie which assembled nightly at the George Inn, on King street. This, however, did not last long, as the late potations and ribald carousings of the company disturbed the entire neighborhood, and attracted attention to the place. The landlord received a stern admonition to keep earlier hours and less uproarious guests. When Boniface sought to carry this admonition into effect Captain Bywater mounted his high horse, and adjourned to his own place, taking his five or six boon companions with him. From that time forward the house on Duchess street was the regular place of meeting.

IV.--THE ORGIES IN THE HOUSE.

Captain Bywater, upon his first arrival at York, had taken up his quarters at a public house. The York inns of the period had an unenviable reputation, and were widely different from the Queen's and Rossin of the present day. Some of my readers will doubtless remember John Gait's savage fling at them several years later. To parody Dr. Johnson's characterization of the famous leg of mutton, they were ill-looking, ill-smelling, ill-provided and ill-kept. In a word, they were unendurable places of sojourn for a man of fastidious tastes and sensitive nerves. Perhaps the Captain's tastes were fastidious, though I can hardly believes that his nerves were sensitive. Possibly he wished to furnish clear evidence that he was no mere sojourner in a strange land, but that he had come here with a view to permanent settlement. At all events his stay at an inn was of brief duration. He rented the house on Duchess street and furnished it in a style which for those days might be called expensive, more especially for a bachelor's establishment. The greater part of the furniture was sent up from Montreal, and the Captain proclaimed his intention of giving a grand house-warming at an early date. He had hardly become settled in the place, however, before his character and antecedent life became known, as already mentioned, and the project was abandoned.

His household consisted of a man-servant named Jim Summers, whom he had picked up at Montreal, and the wife of the latter, who enjoyed the reputation of being an excellent cook, in which capacity she was afterwards employed at the Government House during the regime of Sir John Colborne. At first this couple had a tolerably easy time of it. The Captain was not exigeant, and allowed them to run the establishment pretty much as they chose. He always rose late, and went out immediately after breakfast, accompanied by his large Newfoundland dog Nero, the only living possession he had brought with him from beyond the sea. Master and dog were seen no more until dinner-time, which was five o'clock. Between seven and eight in the evening the pair would betake themselves to the George, where the Captain drank and howled himself hoarse until long past midnight. But he was a seasoned vessel, and generally had pretty fair control over his limbs. He could always find his way home without assistance, and used to direct his man not to wait up for him. The dog was his companion whenever he stirred out of doors.

But when the venue was changed from the tap-room of the George Inn to the Captain's own house, the troubles of Jim Summers and his wife began. The guests commonly arrived within a few minutes of each other, and were all in their places by eight o'clock. They met in the large upper room, and their sessions were prolonged far into the night, or rather into the morning, for it happened often enough that daylight peeped in through the eastern window and found the company still undispersed. Ribald jests, drunken laughter and obscene songs were kept up the whole night through. The quantity of rum, whisky, brandy and beer consumed in the course of a week must have been something to wonder at. The refreshments were provided at the expense of the host, and as it was Jim's business to keep up the supply of spirits, lemons and hot water, he had no sinecure on his hands. It might well be supposed that he might, if so minded, have found a more congenial situation, but as a matter of fact, he was not over scrupulous as to the nature of his employment, and probably had his full share of the fun. The Captain paid good wages, and was lavish in gratuities when he was in good humor. On the whole Jim considered that he had not such a bad place of it, and was by no means disposed to quarrel with his bread and butter. His wife took a different view of affairs, and ere long refused to remain on the premises during the nightly orgies. This difficulty was got over by an arrangement whereby she was permitted to quit the house at eight o'clock in the evening, returning on the following morning in time to prepare the

Captain's breakfast. She spent her nights with a married sister who lived a short distance away, and by this means she avoided what to any woman of respectability must have been an unbearable infliction.

The orgies, in process of time, became a reproach to the neighborhood and a scandal to the town. They were, however, kept up with few interruptions, for several months. More than one townsman declared that so intolerable a nuisance must be abated, but no one liked to be the first to stir in such an unpleasant business, and the bacchanalians continued to "vex with mirth the drowsy ear of night," unchecked by more cleanly-living citizens. But just about the time when these carousings had become absolutely intolerable to the community, they were put a stop to without any outside interference.

V.--THE CATASTROPHE IN THE HOUSE.

On a certain Sunday night, which was destined to be memorable in the annals of the Duchess street house, the number of Captain Bywater's guests was smaller than usual. They consisted of only three persons:

1. Henry John Porter, an articled clerk in the office of Simon Washburn. Mr. Washburn was a well-known lawyer of those times, whose office was on the corner of Duke and George streets. He acted professionally for the Ridout family, and had the letting and sale of the Duchess street property. It was probably through this circumstance that his clerk had become acquainted with Captain Bywater.

2. James McDougall, who was employed in some subordinate capacity in the Civil Service.

3. Alfred Jordan Pilkey, whose occupation seems to have been nothing in particular.

What had become of the other regular attendants does not appear. Not only were the guests few in number on this particular evening, but the proceedings themselves seem to have been of a much less noisy character than ordinary. It was noticed that the host was somewhat out of humor, and that he displayed signs of ill-temper which were not usual with him. His demeanor reflected itself upon his company, and the fun was neither fast nor furious. In fact the time passed somewhat drearily, and the sederunt broke up at the unprecedentedly early hour of eleven o'clock. The man-servant saw the company out, locked the door, and repaired to the room up-stairs where his master still lingered, to see if anything more was required of him.

The Captain sat in a large armchair by the fire, sipping a final glass of grog. He seemed gloomy and dispirited, as though he had something on his mind. In response to Jim's enquiry whether he wanted anything he growled out: "No, go to bed, and be hanged to you." Jim took him at his word, so far as the first clause of the injunction was concerned. He went to bed in his room on the opposite side of the hallway. In passing through the hall he perceived Nero lying asleep on the mat in front of his master's bedroom, which was the small room in the rear of the large apartment where the meetings were held.

Jim had not been in bed many minutes and was in a tranquil state between sleeping and waking, when he heard his master emerge from the front room, and pass along the hallway, as though about to enter his bed-chamber. Another moment and he was roused from his half-somnolent condition by the hearing of the sharp report of a pistol shot, followed by a sound from Nero, something between a moan and a howl. He sprang to the floor, but ere he could make his way into the hall he was well-nigh stunned by hearing a tremendous crash, as though some large body had been hurled violently down the stairs from top to bottom. A vague thought of robbers flashed through his brain, and he paused for a moment, as he himself afterwards admitted, half paralyzed with fright. He called aloud upon his master and then upon the dog, but received no response from either. The crash of the falling body was succeeded by absolute silence. Pulling his nerves together he struck a match, lighted his candle and passed in fear and trembling into the hallway. The first sight that greeted his eyes was the seemingly lifeless body of Nero lying stretched out at the head of the stairs. Upon approaching the body he found blood trickling from a wound in the poor brute's throat. One of the Captain's pistols lay on the floor, close by. But where was the Captain himself? Shading his eyes and holding the candle before him he peered fearfully down the stairway, but the darkness was too profound to admit of his seeing to the bottom. By this time a foreshadowing of the truth had made its way to his understanding. He crept gingerly down the stairs, slowly step by step, holding the candle far in advance, and anon calling upon his master by name. He had passed more than half the way down before he received full confirmation of his forebodings.

There, lying at full length across the hallway, between the foot of the stairs and the front door, was the body of Remy Errington's murderer, with the sinister, evil face turned up to the ceiling. His left arm, still grasping a candlestick, was doubled under him, and his body, in its impetuous descent, had torn away the lower portion of the balustrade. The distraught serving-man raised the head on his arm, and, by such means as occurred to him, sought to ascertain whether any life still lingered there. He could find no pulsation at the wrist, but upon applying his ear to the left side he fancied he could detect a slight fluttering of the heart. Then he rushed to the kitchen, and returned with a pitcher of water, which he dashed in the prostrate face. As this produced no apparent effect he ran back upstairs to his bedroom, threw on part of his clothes, and made his way at full speed to the house of Dr. Pritchard on Newgate street.

The doctor was a late bird, and had not retired to rest. He at once set out for Duchess street, Jim Summers going round by the house of his sister-in-law on Palace street to arouse his wife, who slept there. Upon receiving his wife's promise to follow him as soon as she could huddle on her clothing, Jim ran on in advance, and reached the Duchess street house, only a minute or two later than Dr. Pritchard. The doctor had been there long enough, however, to ascertain that the Captain's neck was broken, and that he was where no human aid could reach him. He would preside over no more orgies in the large room on the upper story.

VI.--THE INQUEST IN THE HOUSE.

There was an inquest. That, under the circumstances, was a matter of course, but nothing of importance was elicited beyond what has already been noted. Porter, Macdougall and Pilkey all attended, and gave evidence to the effect, that Captain Bywater was tolerably drunk when they left him at eleven, but that he was upon the whole the most sober of the party and appeared quite capable of taking care of himself. They had noticed his uncongenial mood, but could afford no conjecture as to the cause. It was impossible to suspect anything in the shape of foul play. The obvious conclusion to be arrived at was that the Captain's long drinking bouts had produced their legitimate result, and that at the moment when he met his death he was suffering from, or on the verge of delirium tremens. He generally carried a loaded pistol in his breast pocket. He had found the dog asleep on the mat before his bedchamber. It was probably asleep, or, at all events, it did not hasten to get out of his way, and in a moment of insane fury or drunken stupidity he had drawn forth his weapon, and shot the poor brute dead. He had just then been standing near the top of the stairs. The quantity of liquor he had drunk was sufficient to justify the conclusion that he was not as steady on his pins as a sober man would have been. He had over-balanced himself, and--and that was the whole story. The coroner's jury brought in a verdict in accordance with the facts, and the Captain's body was put to bed with the sexton's spade.

A will, drawn up in due form in the office of Mr. Washburn, and properly signed and attested, had been made by the deceased a short time after taking possession of the place on Duchess street. His fortune chiefly consisted of an income of five hundred pounds sterling per annum, secured on real estate situated in Gloucestershire, England. This income lapsed upon his death, and it had thus been unnecessary to make any testamentary provision respecting it, except as to the portion which should accrue between the last quarter-day and the death of the testator. This portion was bequeathed to an elder brother residing in Gloucestershire. All the other property of the deceased was bequeathed to Mr. Washburn, in trust to dispose of such personal belongings as did not consist of ready money, and to transmit the proceeds, together with all the cash in hand, to the said elder brother in Gloucestershire.

The latter provisions were duly carried into effect by Mr. Washburn within a few days after the funeral, and it might well have been supposed that the good people of York had heard the last of Captain Bywater and his affairs.

But they hadn't.

VII.--THE BLACK DOG AND HIS MASTER.

At the sale of Captain Bywater's effects a portion of the furniture belonging to the dining-room, kitchen and one bedroom were purchased by Jim Summers, who, with his wife, continued to reside in the Duchess street house pending the letting of it to a new tenant. These temporary occupants thus lived in three rooms, their sleeping apartment being on the upper story at the northern side of the house, and on the opposite side of the hall from the large room which had been the scene of so much recent dissipation. All the rest of the house was left bare, and the doors of the unoccupied rooms were kept locked. Summers found employment as porter and assistant in Hammell's grocery store, but his wife was always on hand to show the premises to anyone who might wish to see them.

All went on quietly until nearly a month after the funeral. Mrs. Summers had an easy time of it, as no intending tenants presented themselves, and her only visitor was her married sister, who occasionally dropped in for an hour's chat. Jim was always at home by seven in the evening, and the time glided by without anything occurring to disturb the smooth current of their lives.

But this state of things was not to be of long continuance. One night when Mr. Washburn was busy over his briefs in his study at home he was disturbed by a loud knocking at his front door. As it was nearly midnight, and as everyone else in the house had retired to rest, he answered the summons in person. Upon unfastening the door he found Jim and his wife at the threshold. They were only half dressed, and their countenances were colorless as Pallida Mors. They stumbled impetuously into the hall, and were evidently laboring under some tremendous excitement. The lawyer conducted them into the study, where they poured into his astonished ears a most singular tale.

Their story was to the effect that they had been disturbed for several nights previously by strange and inexplicable noises in the house occupied by them on Duchess street. They had been aroused from sleep at indeterminate hours by the sound of gliding footsteps just outside of the door of their bedroom. Once they had distinctly heard the sound of voices, which seemed to come from the large front room across the hall. As the door of that room was last closed and locked, they had not been able to distinguish the particular words, but they both declared that the voice was marvellously like that of Captain Bywater. They were persons of fairly steady nerves, but their situation, all things considered, was solitary and peculiar, and they had not by any means relished these unaccountable manifestations. On each occasion, however, they had controlled themselves sufficiently to institute a vigorous investigation of the premises, but had discovered nothing to throw any light upon the subject. They had found all the doors and the windows securely fastened and there was no sign of the presence of anything or anybody to account for the gliding footsteps.

They had unlocked and entered the front room, and found it bare and deserted as it had been left ever since the removal of the furniture after the sale. They had even gone to the length of unlocking and entering every other room in the house, but had found no clue to the mysterious sounds which had disturbed them. Then they had argued themselves into the belief that imagination had imposed upon them, or that there was some natural but undiscovered cause for what had occurred. They were reluctant to make themselves the laughingstock of the town by letting the idea get abroad that they were afraid of ghosts, and they determined to hold their tongues. But the manifestations had at last assumed a complexion which rendered it impossible to pursue such a course any longer, and they vehemently protested that they would not pass another night in the accursed house for any bribe that could be offered them.

They had spent the preceding evening at home, as usual, and had gone to bed a little before ten o'clock. The recent manifestations had probably left some lingering trace upon their nerves, but they had no premonitions of further experiences of the same character, and had soon dropped asleep. They knew not how long they had slept when they were suddenly and simultaneously rendered broad awake by a succession of sounds which could not possibly be explained by any reference to mere imagination. They heard the voice of their late master as distinctly as they had ever heard it during his life. As before, it emanated from the front room, but this time there was no possibility of their being deceived, as they caught not only the sound of his voice, but also certain words which they had often heard from his lips in bygone times. "Don't spare the liquor, gentlemen," roared the Captain, "there's plenty more where that came from. More sugar and lemon, you scoundrel, and be handy there with the hot water." Then was heard the jingling of glasses and loud rapping as if made with the knuckles of the hand upon the table. Other voices were now heard joining in conversation, but too indistinctly for the now thoroughly frightened listeners to catch any of the actual words. There could, however, be no mistake. Captain Bywater had certainly come back from the land of shadows and re-instituted the old orgies in the old spot. The uproar lasted for at least five minutes, when the Captain gave one of his characteristic drunken howls, and of a sudden all was still and silent as the grave.

As might naturally have been expected, the listeners were terror-stricken. For a few moments after the cessation of the disturbance, they lay there in silent, open-mouthed wonderment and fear. Then, before they could find their voices, their ears were assailed by a loud noise in the hall below, followed by the muffled "bow-wow" of a dog, the sound of which seemed to come from the landing at the head of the stairway. Jim could stand the pressure of the situation no longer. He sprang from the bed, lighted a candle, and rushed out into the hall. This he did, as he afterwards admitted, not because he felt brave, but because he was too terrified to remain in bed, and seemed to be impelled by a resolve to face the worst that fate might have in store for him. Just as he passed from the door into the hall, a heavy footstep was heard slowly ascending the stairs. He paused where he stood, candle in hand. The steps came on, on, on, with measured tread. A moment more and he caught sight of the ascending figure. Horror of horrors! It was his late master--clothes, cane and all--just as he had been in life; and at the head of the stairs stood Nero, who gave vent to another low bark of recognition. When the Captain reached the landing place he turned halfway round, and the light of the candle fell full on his face. Jim saw the whole outline with the utmost clearness, even to the expression in the eyes, which was neither gay nor sad, but rather stolid and stern--just what he had been accustomed to see there. The dog crouched back against the wall, and after a brief halt near the stair-head, Captain Bywater turned the knob of his bed-room door and passed in. The dog followed, the door was closed, and once more all was silent. Jim turned and encountered the white face of his wife. She had been standing behind him all the while, and had seen everything just as it had been presented to his own eyes. Moreover, impelled by some inward prompting for which she could never account, she had counted the footsteps as they had ascended the stairs. They had been exactly seventeen!

The pair re-entered their room and took hurried counsel together. They had distinctly seen the Captain turn the knob and pass into his bed-room, followed by the semblance of Nero. As they well knew, the door of that room was locked, and the key was at that moment in the pocket of Mrs. Summers' dress. In sheer desperation they resolved at all hazards to unlock the door and enter the room. Mrs. Summers produced the key and handed it to her husband. She carried the candle and accompanied him to the stair-head. He turned the lock and pushed the door wide open before him, and both advanced into the room. It was empty, and the window was found firmly fastened on the inside, as it had been left weeks before.

They returned to their own bedroom, and agreed that any further stay in such a house of horrors was not to be thought of. Hastily arraying themselves in such clothing as came readily to hand, they passed down the stair-way, unbolted the front door, blew out the light, and made their way into the open air. Then they re-locked the door from outside and left the place. Their intended destination was the house of Mrs. Summers' sister, but they determined to go round by Mr. Washburn's and tell him their story, as they knew he kept late hours and would most likely not have gone to bed.

Mr. Washburn, stolid man of law though he was, could not listen to such a narrative without perceptible signs of astonishment. After thinking over the matter a few moments, he requested his visitors to pass the night under his roof, and to keep their own counsel for the present about their strange experiences. As he well knew, if the singular story got wind there would be no possibility of finding another tenant for the vacant house. The young couple acceded to the first request, and promised compliance with the second. They were then shown to a spare room, and the marvels of that strange night were at an end.

Next morning at an early hour the lawyer and the ex-serving man proceeded to the Duchess street house. Everything was as it had been left the night before, and no clue could be found to the mysterious circumstances so solemnly attested to by Jim Summers and his spouse. The perfect sincerity of the couple could not be doubted, but Mr. Washburn was on the whole disposed to believe that they had in some way been imposed upon by designing persons who wished to frighten them off the premises, or that their imaginations had played them a scurvy trick. With a renewed caution as to silence he dismissed them, and they thenceforth took up their abode in the house of Mrs. Summers' sister on Palace street.

Mr. and Mrs. Summers kept their mouths as close as, under the circumstances, could reasonably have been expected of them. But it was necessary to account in some way for their sudden desertion of the Duchess street house, and Mrs. Summers' sister was of an inquisitive disposition. By degrees she succeeded in getting at most of the facts, but to do her justice she did not proclaim them from the housetops, and for some time the secret was pretty well kept. The story would probably not have become generally known at all, but for a succession of circumstances which took place when the haunted house had been vacant about two months.

An American immigrant named Horsfall arrived at York with a view of settling there and opening out a general store. He was a man of family and of course required a house to live in. It so happened that the store rented to him on King street had no house attached to it, and it was therefore necessary for him to look out for a suitable place elsewhere. Hearing that a house on Duchess street was to let, he called and went over the premises with Mr. Washburn, who naturally kept silent as to the supernatural appearances which had driven the Summerses from the door in the middle of the night. The inspection proved satisfactory, and Mr. Horsfall took the place for a year. His household consisted of his wife, two grown-up daughters, a son in his fifteenth year, and a black female servant. They came up from Utica in advance of Mr. Horsfall's expectations, and before the house was ready for them, but matters were pushed forward with all possible speed, and on the evening of the second day after their arrival they took possession of the place. The furniture was thrown in higgledy-piggledy, and all attempts to put things to rights were postponed until the next day. The family walked over after tea from the inn at which they had been staying, resolving to rough it for a single night in their new home in preference to passing another night amid countless swarms of "the pestilence that walketh in darkness." Two beds were hastily made up on the floor of the drawing-room, one for the occupation of Mr. and Mrs. Horsfall, and the other for the two young women. A third bed was hastily extemporized on the floor of the dining-room for the occupation of Master George Washington, and Dinah found repose on a lounge in the adjacent kitchen. The entire household went to bed sometime between ten and eleven o'clock, all pretty well tired, and prepared for a comfortable night's rest. They had been in bed somewhat more than an hour when the whole family was aroused by the barking of a dog in the lower hall. This was, not unnaturally, regarded as strange, inasmuch as all the doors and windows had been carefully fastened by Mr. Horsfall before retiring, and there had certainly been no dog in the house then. The head of the family lost no time in lighting a candle and opening the door into the hall. At the same moment young G. W. opened the door on the opposite side. Yes, there, sure enough, was a large, black Newfoundland dog, seemingly very much at home, as though he belonged to the place. As the youth advanced towards him he retreated to the stairway, up which he passed at a great padding pace. How on earth had he gained an entrance? Well, at all events he must be got rid of; but he looked as if he would be an awkward customer to tackle at close quarters and Mr. Horsfall deemed it prudent to put on a part of his clothing before making any attempt to expel him. While he was dressing, the tread of the animal on the floor of the upper hall could be distinctly heard, and ever and anon he emitted a sort of low, barking sound, which was ominous of a disposition to resent any interference with him. By this time all the members of the household were astir and clustering about the lower hall. Mr. Horsfall, with a lighted candle in one hand and a stout cudgel in the other, passed up the stairs and looked along the passage. Why, what on earth had become of the dog! It was nowhere to be seen! Where could it have hidden itself? It was certainly too large an animal to have taken refuge in a rathole. Had it entered one of the rooms? Impossible, for they were all closed, though not locked. Mr. H. himself having unlocked them in the course of the afternoon, when some furniture had been taken into them. He, however, looked into each room in succession, only to find "darkness there and nothing more." Then he concluded that the brute must have gone down stairs while he had been putting on his clothes in the room below. No, that could not be, for George Washington had never left the foot of the stairway from the moment the dog first passed up. Had it jumped through one of the windows? No, they were all fast and intact. Had it gone up the chimney of the front room? No; apart from the absurdity of the idea, the hole was not large enough to admit of a dog one-fifth its size. In vain the house was searched through and through. Not a sign of the huge disturber of the domestic peace was to be seen anywhere.

After a while, Mr. Horsfall, at a loss for anything better to exercise his faculties upon, opened both the front and back doors and looked all over the premises, alternately calling Carlo! Watch! and every other name which occurred to him as likely to be borne by a dog. There was no response, and in sheer disgust he re-entered the house and again sought his couch. In a few minutes more the household was again locked in slumber. But they were not at the end of their annoyances. About half an hour after midnight they were once more aroused.--this time by the sound of loud voices in the large upper room. "I tell you we will all have glasses round," roared a stentorian voice--"I will knock down the first man who objects!" Everybody in the house heard the voice and the words. This was apparently more serious than the dog. Mr. H. regretted that he had left his pistols at the inn, but he determined to rid the place of the intruders whoever they might be. Grasping the cudgel he again made his way up-stairs, candle in hand. When more than half way up he caught sight of a tall, heavily-built, red-faced man, who had apparently emerged from the larger room, and who was just on the point of opening the door of the back bed-room. "Who are you, you scoundrel?" exclaimed Mr. H. The man apparently neither saw nor heard him, but opened the door with tranquil unconcern and passed into the room. Mr. H. followed quickly at his very heels--only to find that he had been beguiled with a counterfeit, and that there was no one there. Then he stepped back into the hallway, and entered the larger room with cudgel raised, fully expecting to find several men there. To his unspeakable astonishment he found nobody. Again he hurried from room to room, upstairs and downstairs. Again he examined the doors and windows to see if the fastenings had been tampered with. No, all was tight and snug. The family were again astir, hurrying hither and thither, in quest of they knew not what; but they found nothing to reward their search, and after a while all gathered together half-clad in the dining room, where they began to ask each other what these singular disturbances could mean.

Mr. Horsfall was a plain, matter of fact personage, and up to this moment no idea of any supernatural visitation had so much as entered his mind. Even now he scouted the idea when it was timidly broached by his wife. He, however, perceived plainly enough that this was something altogether out of the common way, and he announced his intention of going to bed no more that night. The others lay down again, but we may readily believe that they slept lightly, if at all, though nothing more occurred to disturb them. Soon after daylight all the family rose and dressed for the day. Once more they made tour after tour through all the rooms, only to find that everything remained precisely as it had been left on the preceding night.

After an early breakfast Mr. H. proceeded to the house of Mr. Washburn, where he found that gentleman was still asleep, and that he could not be disturbed. The visitor was a patient man and declared his intention of waiting. In about an hour Mr. Washburn came down stairs, and heard the extraordinary story which his tenant had to relate. He had certainly not anticipated anything of this sort, and gave vehement utterance to his surprise. In reply to Mr. H.'s enquiries about the house, however, he gave him a brief account of the life and death of Captain Bywater, and supplemented the biography by a narration of the singular experiences of Jim Summers and his wife. Then the American fired up, alleging that his landlord had had no right to let him the house, and to permit him to remove his family into it, without acquainting him with the facts beforehand. The lawyer admitted that he had perhaps been to blame, and expressed his regret. The tenant declared that he then and there threw up his tenancy, and that he would vacate the house in the course of the day. Mr. Washburn felt that a court of law would probably hesitate to enforce a lease under such circumstances, and assented that the arrangement between them should be treated as cancelled.

VIII.--THE LAST OF THE HOUSE.

And cancelled it was. Mr. Horsfall temporarily took his family and his other belongings back to the inn, but soon afterwards secured a house where no guests, canine, or otherwise, were in the habit of intruding themselves uninvited in the silent watches of the night. He kept a store here for some years, and, I believe, was buried at York. A son of his, as I am informed--probably the same who figures in the foregoing narrative--is, or lately was, a well-to-do resident of Syracuse, N. Y.

Mr. Horsfall made no secret of his reasons for throwing up his tenancy, and his adventures were soon noised abroad throughout the town. He was the last tenant of the sombre house. Thenceforward no one could be induced to rent it or even to occupy it rent free. It was commonly regarded as a whisht, gruesome spot, and was totally unproductive to its owners. Its subsequent history has already been given.

And now what more is there to tell? Only this: that the main facts of the foregoing story are true. Of course I am not in a position to vouch for them from personal knowledge, any more than I am in a position to personally vouch for the invasion of England by William of Normandy. But they rest on as good evidence as most other private events of sixty-odd years ago, and there is no reason for doubting their literal truth. With regard to the supernatural element, I am free to confess that I am not able to accept it in entirety. This is not because I question the veracity of those who vouch for the alleged facts, but because I have not received those facts at first hand, and because I am not very ready to believe in the supernatural at all. I think that, in the case under consideration, an intelligent investigation at the time might probably have brought to light circumstances as to which the narrative, as it stands, is silent. Be that as it may, the tale is worth the telling, and I have told it.

SAVAREEN'S DISAPPEARANCE.

A HALF-FORGOTTEN CHAPTER IN THE HISTORY OF AN UPPER CANADIAN TOWNSHIP.

CHAPTER I.
THE PLACE AND THE MAN.

Near the centre of one of the most flourishing of the western counties of Ontario, and on the line of the Great Western branch of the Grand Trunk Railway, stands a pleasant little town, which, for the purposes of this narrative, may be called Millbrook. Not that its real name is Millbrook, or any thing in the least similar thereto; but as this story, so far as its main events are concerned, is strictly true, and some of the actors in it are still living, it is perhaps desirable not to be too precise in the matter of locality. The strange disappearance of Mr. Savareen made a good deal of noise at the time, not only in the neighborhood, but throughout Upper Canada. It was a nine days' wonder, and was duly chronicled and commented upon by the leading provincial newspapers of the period; but it has long since passed out of general remembrance, and the chain of circumstances subsequently arising out of the event have never been made known beyond the limited circle immediately interested. The surviving members of that circle would probably not thank me for once more dragging their names conspicuously before the public gaze. I might certainly veil their personalities under the thin disguise of initial letters, but to this mode of relating a story I have always entertained a decided objection. The chief object to be aimed at in story-telling is to hold the attention of the reader, and, speaking for myself, I am free to confess that I have seldom been able to feel any absorbing interest in characters who figure merely as the M. or N. of the baptismal service. I shall therefore assign fictitious names to persons and places, and I cannot even pretend to mathematical exactness as to one or two minor details. In reporting conversations, for instance, I do not profess to reproduce the ***ipsissima verba*** of the speakers, but merely to give the effect and purport of their discourses. I have, however, been at some pains to be accurate, and I think I may justly claim that in all essential particulars this story of Savareen's disappearance is as true as any report of events which took place a good many years ago can reasonably be expected to be.

First: As to the man. Who was he?

Well, that is easily told. He was the second son of a fairly well-to-do English yeoman, and had been brought up to farming pursuits on the paternal acres in Hertfordshire. He emigrated to Upper Canada in or about the year 1851, and had not been many weeks in the colony before he became the tenant of a small farm situated in the township of Westchester, three miles to the north of Millbrook. At that time he must have been about twenty-five or twenty-six years of age. So far as could be judged by those who came most frequently into personal relations with him, he had no very marked individuality to distinguish him from others of his class and station in life. He was simply a young English farmer who had migrated to Canada with a view to improving his condition and prospects.

In appearance he was decidedly prepossessing. He stood five feet eleven inches in his stockings; was broad of shoulder, strong of arm, and well set up about the limbs. His complexion was fair and his hair had a decided inclination to curl. He was proficient in most athletics; could box and shoot, and if put upon his mettle, could leap bodily over a five-barred gate. He was fond of good living, and could always be depended upon to do full justice to a well-provided dinner. It cannot be denied that he occasionally drank more than was absolutely necessary to quench a normal thirst, but he was as steady as could be expected of any man who has from his earliest boyhood been accustomed to drink beer as an ordinary beverage, and has always had the run of the buttery hatch. He liked a good horse, and could ride anything that went on four legs. He also had a weakness for dogs, and usually had one or two of those animals dangling near his heels whenever he stirred out of doors. Men and things in this country were regarded by him from a strictly trans-Atlantic point of view, and he was frequently heard to remark that this, that, and the other thing were "nothink to what we 'ave at 'ome."

He was more or less learned in matters pertaining to agriculture, and knew something about the current doctrines bearing on the rotation of crops. His literary education, moreover, had not been wholly neglected. He could read and write, and could cast up accounts which were not of too involved and complicated a character. It cannot truly be said that he had read Tom Jones, Roderick Random, and Pierce Egan's Life in London. He regarded Cruikshank's illustrations to the last named work--more particularly that one depicting Corinthian Tom "getting the best of Charley,"--as far better worth looking at than the whole collection in the National Gallery, a place where he had once whirled away a tedious hour or two during a visit to town.

Then, he was not altogether ignorant concerning several notable events in the history of his native land. That is to say, he knew that a certain king named Charles the First had been beheaded a good many years ago, and that a disreputable person-age named Oliver Cromwell had somehow been mixed up in the transaction. He understood that the destinies of Great Britain were presided over by Queen Victoria and two Houses of Parliament, called respectively the House of Lords and the House of Commons; and he had a sort of recollection of having heard that those august bodies were called Estates of the Realm. In his eyes, everything English was *ipso facto* to be commended and admired, whereas everything un-English was *ipso fac-to* to be proportionately condemned and despised. Any misguided person who took a different view of the matter was to be treated as one who had denied the faith, and was worse than an infidel.

I have said that his appearance was prepossessing, and so it was in the ordinary course of things, though he had a broad scar on his left cheek, which, on the rare oc-casions when he was angry, asserted itself somewhat conspicuously, and imparted, for the nonce, a sinister expression to his countenance. This disfigurement, as I have heard, had been received by him some years before his arrival in Canada. During a visit to one of the market towns in the neighborhood of his home, he had casually dropped into a gymnasium, and engaged in a fencing bout with a friend who accompanied him. Neither of the contestants had ever handled a foil before, and they were of course unskilled in the use of such dangerous playthings. During the contest the button had slipped from his opponent's weapon, just as the latter was making a vigorous lunge. As a consequence Savareen's cheek had been laid open by a wound which left its permanent impress upon him. He himself was in the habit of jocularly alluding to this disfigurement as his "bar sinister."

For the rest, he was stubborn as a mule about trifles which did not in the least concern him, but as regarded the affairs of every-day life he was on the whole pleasant and easy-going, more especially when nothing occurred to put him out. When anything of the kind *did* occur, he could certainly assume the attitude of an ugly customer, and on such occasions the wound on his cheek put on a lurid hue which was not pleasant to contemplate. His ordinary discourse mainly dealt with the events of his everyday life. It was not intellectually stimulating, and for the most part related to horses, dogs, and the crop prospects of the season. In short, if you have ever lived in rural England, or if you have been in the habit of frequenting English country towns on market-days, you must have encountered scores of jolly young farmers who, to all outward seeming, with the solitary exception of the sinister scar, might pretty nearly have stood for his portrait.

Such was Reginald Bourchier Savareen, and if you have never come across anybody possessing similar characteristics--always excepting the scar-- your experience of your fellow-creatures has been more limited than might be expected from a reader of your age and manifest intelligence.

His farm--*i.e.*, the farm rented by him--belonged to old Squire Harrington, and lay in a pleasant valley on the western side of the gravel road leading northward from Millbrook to Spotswood. The Squire himself lived in the red brick mansion which peeped out from the clump of maples a little further down on the opposite side of the road. The country thereabouts was settled by a thrifty and prosperous race of pioneers, and presented a most attractive appearance. Alternate successions of hill and dale greeted the eye of the traveller as he drove along the hard-packed highway, fifteen miles in length, which formed the connecting link between the two towns above mentioned. The land was carefully tilled, and the houses, generally speaking, were of a better class than were to be found in most rural communities in Upper Canada at that period. Savareen's own dwelling was unpretentious enough, having been originally erected for one of the squire's "hired men," but it was sufficient for his needs, as he had not married until a little more than a year before the happening of the events to be presently related, and his domestic establishment was small. His entire household consisted of himself, his young wife, an infant in arms, a man servant and a rustic maid of all work. In harvest time he, of course, employed additional help, but the harvesters were for the most part residents of the neighborhood, who found accommodation in their own homes. The house was a small frame, oblong building, of the conventional Canadian farm-house order of architecture, painted of a drab color and standing a hundred yards or so from the main road. The barn and stable stood a convenient distance to the rear. About midway between house and barn was a deep well, worked with a windlass and chain. During the preceding season a young orchard had been planted out in the space intervening between the house and the road. Everything about the place was kept in spick and span order. The tenant was fairly successful in his farming operations, and appeared to be holding his own with the world around him. He paid his rent promptly, and was on excellent terms with his landlord. He was, in fact, rather popular with his neighbors generally, and was regarded as a man with a fair future before him.

CHAPTER II.
THE NEIGHBORHOOD.

About a quarter of a mile to the north of Savareen's abode was a charming little hostelry, kept by a French Canadian named Jean Baptiste Lapierre. It was one of the snuggest and cosiest of imaginable inns; by no means the sort of wayside tavern commonly to be met with in Western Canada in those times, or even in times much more recent. The landlord had kept a high-class restaurant in Quebec in the old days before the union of the Provinces, and piqued himself upon knowing what was what. He was an excellent cook, and knew how to cater to the appetites of more exacting epicures than he was likely to number among his ordinary patrons in a rural community like that in which he had piched his quarters. When occasion required, he could serve up a dinner or supper at which Brillat Savarian himself would have had no excuse for turning up his nose. It was seldom that any such exigeant demand as this was made upon his skill, but even his ordinary fare was good enough for any city sir or madam whom chance might send beneath his roof, and such persons never failed to carry away with them pleasant remembrances of the place.

The creaking sign which swayed in the breeze before the hospitable door proclaimed it to be The Royal Oak, but it was commonly known throughout the whole of that country-side as Lapierre's. The excellence of its larder was proverbial, insomuch that professional men and others used frequently to drive out from town expressly to dine or sup there. Once a week or so--usually on Saturday nights--a few of the choice spirits thereabouts used to meet in the cosy parlor and hold a decorous sort of free-and-easy, winding up with supper at eleven o'clock. On these occasions, as a matter of course, the liquor flowed with considerable freedom, and the guests had a convivial time of it; but there was nothing in the shape of wild revelry--nothing to bring reproach upon the good name of the house. Jean Baptiste had too much regard for his well-earned reputation to permit these meetings to degenerate into mere orgies. He showed due respect for the sanctity of the Sabbath, and took care to make the house clear of company before the stroke of midnight. By such means he not only kept his guests from indulging in riotous excesses, but secured their respect for himself and his establishment.

Savareen was a pretty regular attendant at these convivial gatherings, and was indeed a not infrequent visitor at other times. He always met with a warm welcome, for he could sing a good song, and paid his score with commendable regularity. His Saturday nights' potations did not interfere with his timely appearance on Sunday morning in his pew in the little church which stood on the hill a short distance above Lapierre's. His wife usually sat by his side, and accompanied him to and fro. Everything seemed to indicate that the couple lived happily together, and that they were mutually blessed in their domestic relations. With regard to Mrs. Savareen, the only thing necessary to be mentioned about her at present is that she was the daughter of a carpenter and builder resident in Millbrook.

There was a good deal of travel on the Millbrook and Spotswood road, more especially in the autumn, when the Dutch farmers from the settlements up north used to come down in formidable array, for the purpose of supplying themselves with fruit to make cider and "applesass" for the winter. The great apple-producing district of the Province begins in the townships lying a few miles to the south of Westchester, and the road between Millbrook and Spotswood was, and is, the most direct route thither from the Dutch settlements. The garb and other appointments of the stalwart Canadian Teuton of those days were such as to make him easily distinguishable from his Celtic or Saxon neighbor. He usually wore a long, heavy, coat of coarse cloth, reaching down to his heels. His head was surmounted by a felt hat with a brim wide enough to have served, at a pinch, for the tent of a side-show. His wagon was a great lumbering affair, constructed, like himself, after an ante-diluvian pattern, and pretty nearly capacious enough for a first-rate man-of-war. In late September and early October it was no unprecedented thing to see as many as thirty or forty of these ponderous vehicles moving southward, one at the tail of the other, in a continuous string. They came down empty, and returned a day or two afterwards laden with the products of the southern orchards. On the return journey the wagons were full to overflowing. Not so the drivers, who were an exceedingly temperate and abstemious people, too parsimonious to leave much of their specie at the Royal Oak. It was doubtless for this reason that mine host Lapierre regarded, and was accustomed to speak of them with a good deal of easy contempt, not to say aversion. They brought little or no grist to his mill, and he was fond of proclaiming that he did not keep a hotel for the accommodation of such *canaille*. The emphasis placed by him on this last word was something quite refreshing to hear.

The road all the way from Millbrook to Spotswood, corresponds to the mathematical definition of a straight line. It forms the third concession of the township, and there is not a curve in it anywhere. The concessions number from west to east, and the sidelines, running at right angles to them are exactly two miles apart. At the northwestern angle formed by the intersection of the gravel road with the first side line north of Millbrook stood a little toll-gate, kept, at the period of the story, by one Jonathan Perry. Between the toll-gate and Savareen's on the same side of the road were several other houses to which no more particular reference is necessary. On the opposite side of the highway, somewhat more than a hundred yards north of the toll-gate, was the abode of a farmer named Mark Stolliver. Half a mile further up was John Calder's house, which was the only one until you came to Squire

Harrington's. To the rear of the Squire's farm was a huge morass about fifty acres in extent, where cranberries grew in great abundance, from which circumstance it was known as Cranberry Swamp.

Now you have the entire neighborhood before you, and if you will cast your eye on the following rough plan you will have no difficulty in taking in the scene at a single glance:--

CHAPTER III.
A JOURNEY TO TOWN.

In the early spring of the year 1854 a letter reached Savareen from his former home in Hertfordshire, containing intelligence of the sudden death of his father. The old gentleman had been tolerably well off in this world's gear, but he had left a numerous family behind him, so that there was no great fortune in store for Reginald. The amount bequeathed to him, however, was four hundred pounds sterling clear of all deductions--a sum not to be despised, as it would go far toward enabling him to buy the farm on which he lived, and would thus give a material impetus to his fortunes. The executors lost no time in winding up and distributing the estate, and during the second week in July a letter arrived from their solicitors enclosing a draft on the Toronto agency of the Bank of British North America for the specified sum. Savareen made arrangements with the local bank at Millbank to collect the proceeds, and thus save him the expense of a journey to Toronto. Meanwhile he concluded a bargain with Squire Harrington for the purchase of the farm. The price agreed upon was $3,500, half of which was to be paid down upon the delivery of the deed, the balance being secured by mortgage. The cash would be forthcoming at the bank not later than the 18th of the month, and accordingly that was the date fixed upon for the completion of the transaction. Lawyer Miller was instructed to have the documents ready for execution at noon, when the parties and their respective wives were to attend at his office in Millbrook.

The morning of Monday, the 17th, was wet and gave promise of a rainy day. As there seemed to be no prospect of his being able to do any outside work on the farm, Savareen thought he might as well ride into town and ascertain if the money had arrived. He saddled his black mare, and started for Millbrook--about ten in the forenoon. His two dogs showed a manifest desire to accompany him, but he did not think fit to gratify their desire and ordered them back. Before he had ridden far the rain ceased, and the sun came out warm and bright, but he was in an idle mood, and didn't think it worth while to turn back. It seems probable indeed, that he had merely wanted an excuse for an idle day in town; as there was no real necessity for such a journey. Upon reaching the front street he stabled his mare at the Peacock Inn, which was his usual house of call when in Millbrook. He next presented himself at the bank, where he made enquiry about his draft. Yes, the funds were there all right. The clerk, supposing that he wanted to draw the amount there and then, counted the notes out for him, and requested him to sign the receipt in the book kept for such purposes. Savareen then intimated that he had merely called to enquire about the matter, and that he wished to leave the money until next day. The clerk, who was out of humor about some trifle or other, and who was, moreover, very busy that morning, spoke up sharply, remarking that he had had more bother about that draft than the transaction was worth. His irritable turn and language nettled Savareen, who accordingly took the notes, signed the receipt and left the bank, declaring that "that shop" should be troubled by no further business of his. The clerk, as soon as he had time to think over the matter, perceived that he had been rude, and would have tendered an apology, but his customer had already shaken the dust of the bank off his feet and taken his departure, so that there was no present opportunity of accommodating the petty quarrel. As events subsequently turned out it was destined never to be accommodated in this world, for the two never met again on this side the grave.

Instead of returning home immediately as he ought to have done, Savareen hung about the tavern all day, drinking more than was good for his constitution, and regaling every boon companion he met with an account of the incivility to which he had been subjected at the hands of the bank clerk. Those to whom he told the story thought he attached more importance to the affair than it deserved, and they noticed that the scar on his cheek came out in its most lurid aspect. He dined at the Peacock and afterwards indulged in sundry games of bagatelle and ten-pins; but the stakes consisted merely of beer and cigars, and he did not get rid of more than a few shillings in the course of the afternoon. Between six and seven in the evening his landlady regaled him with a cup of strong tea, after which he seemed none the worse for his afternoon's relaxations. A few minutes before dusk he mounted his mare and started on his way homeward.

The ominous clouds of the early morning had long since passed over. The sun had shone brightly throughout the afternoon, and had gone down amid a gorgeous blaze of splendour. The moon would not rise till nearly nine, but the evening was delightfully calm and clear, and the horseman's way home was as straight as an arrow, over one of the best roads in the country.

CHAPTER IV.
GONE.

At precisely eight o'clock in the evening of this identical Monday, July 17th, 1854, old Jonathan Perry sat tranquilly smoking his pipe at the door of the toll-gate two miles north of Millbrook.

The atmosphere was too warm to admit of the wearing of any great display of apparel, and the old man sat hatless and coatless on a sort of settle at the threshold. He was an inveterate old gossip, and was acquainted with the business of everybody in the neighborhood. He knew all about the bargain entered into between Savareen and Squire Harrington, and how it was to be consummated on the following day. Savareen, when riding townwards that morning, had informed him of the ostensible purpose of his journey, and it now suddenly occurred to the old man to wonder why the young farmer had not returned home.

While he sat there pondering, the first stroke of the town bell proclaiming the hour was borne upon his ear. Before the ringing had ceased, he caught the additional sound of a horse's hoofs rapidly advancing up the road.

"Ah," said he to himself, "here he comes. I reckon his wife'll be apt to give him fits for being so late."

In another moment the horseman drew up before him, but only to exchange a word of greeting, as the gate was thrown wide open, and there was nothing to bar his progress. The venerable gate-keeper had conjectured right. It was Savareen on his black mare.

"Well, Jonathan, a nice evening," remarked the young farmer.

"Yes, Mr. Savareen--a lovely night. You've had a long day of it in town. They'll be anxious about you at home. Did you find the money all right, as you expected?"

"O, the money was there, right enough, and I've got it in my pocket. I had some words with that conceited puppy, Shuttleworth, at the bank. He's altogether too big for his place, and I can tell you he'll have the handling of no more money of mine." And then, for about the twentieth time within the last few hours, he recounted the particulars of his interview with the bank clerk.

The old man expressed his entire concurrence in Savareen's estimate of Shuttleworth's conduct. "I have to pay the gate-money into the bank on the first of every month," he remarked, "and that young feller always acts as if he felt too uppish to touch it. I wonder you didn't drop into 'un."

"O, I wasn't likely to do that," was the reply--"but I gave him a bit of my mind, and I told him it 'ud be a long time afore I darkened the doors of his shop again. And so it will. I'd sooner keep my bit o' money, when I have any, in the clock-case at home. There's never any housebreaking hereabouts."

Jonathan responded by saying that, in so far as he knew, there hadn't been a burglary for many a year.

"But all the same," he continued, "I shouldn't like to keep such a sum as four hundred pound about me, even for a single night. No more I shouldn't like to carry such a pot o' money home in the night time, even if nobody knew as I had it on me. Ride you home, Mr. Savareen, and hide it away in some safe place till to-morrow morning--that's *my* advice."

"And very good advice it is, Jonathan," was the response. "I'll act upon it without more words. Good night!" And so saying, Savareen continued his course homeward at a brisk trot.

The old man watched him as he sped away up the road, but could not keep him in view more than half a minute or so, as by this time the light of day had wholly departed. He lighted his pipe, which had gone out during the conversation, and resumed his seat on the settle. Scarcely had he done so ere he heard the clatter of horse's hoofs moving rapidly towards the gate from the northward. "Why," said he to himself, "this must be Savareen coming back again. What's the matter now, I wonder?"

But this time he was out in his conjecture. When the horseman reached the gate, he proved to be not Savareen, but mine host Lapierre, mounted on his fast-trotting nag, Count Frontenac--a name irreverently abbreviated by the sportsmen of the district into "Fronty." The rider drew up with a boisterous "Woa!" and reached out towards the gate-keeper a five-cent piece by way of toll, saying as he did so:

"Vell, Mister Perry, how coes everytings wiss you?"

"O, good evening, Mr. Lapierre; I didn't know you till you spoke. My eyesight's getting dimmer every day, I think. Bound for town?"

"Yes, I want to see what has cot Mr. Safareen. He went to town early this morning to see about some money matters, and promised to pe pack in a couple of hours, put he ain't pack yet. Mrs. Safareen cot so uneasy apout him to-night, that she came up to my place and pegged me to ride down and hunt him up. I suppose you saw him on his way down?"

"Saw him! On his way down! What are you talking about? Didn't you meet him just now?"

"Meet who?"

"Savareen."

"Where? When?"

"Why, not two minutes ago. He passed through here on his way home just before you came up."

"How long pefore?"

"How long! Why, don't I tell you, not two minutes. He hadn't hardly got out o' sight when I heerd your horse's feet on the stones, and thought it was him a-coming back again. You must a met him this side o' Stolliver's."

Then followed further explanations on the part of old Jonathan, who recounted the conversation he had just had with Savareen.

Well, of course, the key to the situation was not hard to find. Savareen had left the toll-gate and proceeded northward not more than two or three minutes before Lapierre, riding southward along the same road, had reached the same point. The two had not encountered each other. Therefore, one of them had deviated from the road. There had been no deviation on the part of Lapierre, so the deviator must necessarily have been Savareen. But the space of time which had elapsed was too brief to admit of the latter's having ridden more than a hundred yards or thereabouts.

The only outlet from the road within four times that distance was the gateway leading into Stolliver's house. The explanation, consequently, was simple enough. Savareen had called in at Stollivers. Q. E. D.

Strange, though, that he had said nothing to old Jonathan about his intention to call there. He had ridden off as though intent upon getting home without delay, and hiding his money away in a safe place for the night. And, come to think of it, it was hard to understand what possible reason he could have for calling at Stolliver's. He had never had any business or social relations of any kind with Stolliver, and in fact the two had merely a nodding acquaintance. Still another strange thing was that Savareen should have taken his horse inside the gate, as there was a tying-post outside, and he could not have intended to make any prolonged stay. However, there was no use raising difficult problems, which could doubt less be solved by a moment's explanation. It was absolutely certain that Savareen was at Stolliver's because he could not possibly have avoided meeting Lapierre if he had not called there. It was Lapierre's business to find him and take him home. Accordingly the landlord of the Royal Oak turned his horse's head and cantered back up the road till he reached the front of Stolliver's place.

Stolliver and his two boys were sitting out on the front fence, having emerged from the house only a moment before. They had been working in the fields until past sundown, and had just risen from a late supper. Old Stolliver was in the habit of smoking a pipe every night after his evening meal, and in pleasant weather he generally chose to smoke it out of doors, as he was doing this evening, although the darkness had fallen. Lapierre, as he drew rein, saw the three figures on the fence, but could not in the darkness, distinguish one from, another.

"Is that Mister Stollifer?" he asked.

"Yes; who be *you*?" was the ungracious response, delivered in a gruff tone of voice. Old Stolliver was a boorish, cross-grained customer, who paid slight regard to the amenities, and did not show to advantage in conversation.

"Don't you know me? I am Mister Lapierre."

"O, Mr. Lapierre, eh? Been a warm day."

"Yes. Hass Mister Safareen gone?"

"Mister who?"

"Mister Safareen. Wass he not here shoost now?"

"Here? What fur?"

The landlord was by this time beginning to feel a little disgusted at the man's boorish incivility. "Will you pe so coot as to tell me," he asked, "if Mister Safareen hass peen here?"

"Not as I know of. Hain't seen him."

Lapierre was astounded. He explained the state of affairs to his interlocuter, who received the communication with his wonted stolidity, and proceeded to light his pipe, as much as to say that the affair was none of his funeral.

"Well," he remarked, with exasperating coolness, "I guess you must 'a' passed him on the road. We hain't been out here more'n a minute or two. Nobody hain't passed since then."

This seemed incredible. Where, then, was Savareen? Had he sunk into the bowels of the earth, or gone up, black mare and all, in a balloon? Of course it was all nonsense about the landlord having passed him on the road without seeing or hearing anything of him. But what other explanation did the circumstances admit of? At any rate, there was nothing for Lapierre to do but ride back to Savareen's house and see if he had arrived there. Yes, one other thing might be done. He might return to the toll gate and ascertain whether Jonathan Perry was certain as to the identity of the man from whom he had parted a few minutes before. So Count Frontenac's head was once more turned southward. A short trot brought him again to the toll-house. The gatekeeper was still sitting smoking at the door. A moment's conference with him was sufficient to convince Lapierre that there could be no question of mistaken identity. "Why," said Jonathan, "I know Mr. Savareen as well as I know my right hand. And then, didn't he tell me about his row with Shuttleworth, and that he had the four hundred pounds in his pocket. Why, dark as it was, I noticed the scar on his cheek when he was talking about it.--I say, Missus, look here," he called in a louder tone, whereupon his wife presented herself at the threshold. "Now," resumed the old man, "just tell Mr. Lapierre whether you saw Mr. Savareen talking to me a few minutes since, and whether you saw him ride off up the road just before Mr. Lapierre came down. Did you, or did you not?"

Mrs. Perry's answer was decisive, and at the same time conclusive as to the facts. She had not only seen Savareen sitting on his black mare at the door, immediately after the town bell ceased ringing for eight o'clock; but she had listened to the conversation between him and her husband, and had heard pretty nearly every word. Lapierre cross examined her, and found that her report of the interview exactly corresponded with what he had already heard from old Jonathan. "Why," said she, "there is no more doubt of its being Mr. Savareen than there is of that gate-post being there on the road-side. 'Very good advice it is,' says he, 'and I'll act upon it without more words.' Then he said 'good night,' and off he went up the road. Depend upon it, Mr. Lapierre, you've missed him somehow in the darkness, and he's safe and sound at home by this time."

"Yes, yes, Mr. Lapierre, not a doubt on it," resumed old Jonathan, "you've a passed him on the road athout seein' 'im. It was dark, and you were both in a hurry. I've heerd o' lots o' stranger things nor that."

Lapierre couldn't see it. He knew well enough that it was no more possible for him to pass a man on horseback on that narrow highway, on a clear night, without seeing him--more especially when he was out for the express purpose of finding that very man--than it was possible for him to serve out *un petit verre* of French brandy in mistake for a gill of Hollands. The facts, however, seemed to be wholly against him, as he bade the old couple a despondent good-night and put Count Frontenac to his mettle. He stayed not for brook--there *was* a brook a short distance up the road--and he stopped not for stone, but tore along at a break-neck pace as though he was riding for a wager. In five minutes he reached Savareen's front gate.

Mrs. Savareen was waiting there, on the look-out for her husband. No, of course he had not got home. She had neither seen nor heard anything of him, and was by this time very uneasy. You may be sure that her anxiety was not lessened when she heard the strange tale which Lapierre had to tell her.

Even then, however, she did not give up the hope of her husband's arrival sometime during the night. Lapierre promised to look in again in an hour or two, and passed on to his own place, where he regaled the little company he found there with the narrative of his evening's exploits. Before bedtime the story was known all over the neighborhood.

CHAPTER V.
ONE HUNDRED POUNDS REWARD.

Mrs. Savareen sat up waiting for her lord until long past midnight, but her vigil was in vain. Lapierre, after closing up his inn for the night, dropped in, according to his promise, to see if any news of the absentee had arrived. Nothing further could be done in the way of searching for the latter personage until daylight.

It was getting on pretty well towards morning when Mrs. Savareen sought her couch, and when she got there her slumber was broken and disturbed. She knew not what to think, but she was haunted by a dread that she would never again see her husband alive.

Next morning, soon after daylight, the whole neighborhood was astir, and the country round was carefully searched for any trace of the missing man. Squire Harrington went down to town and made inquiries at the bank, where he ascertained that the story told by Savareen to old Jonathan Perry, as to his altercation with Shuttleworth, was substantially correct. This effectually disposed of any possible theory as to Jonathan and his wife having mistaken somebody else for Savareen. Squire Harrington likewise learned all about the man's doings on the previous afternoon, and was able to fix the time at which he had started for home. He had ridden from the door of the Peacock at about a quarter to eight. This would bring him to the toll-gate at eight o'clock--the hour at which Perry professed to have seen and conversed with him. There was no longer any room for doubt. That interview and conversation had actually taken place at eight o'clock on the previous evening, and Savareen had ridden northward from the gate within five minutes afterwards. He could not have proceeded more than a hundred--or, at the very outside, two hundred--yards further, or he must inevitably have been encountered by Lapierre. How had he contrived to vanish so suddenly out of existence? And it was not only the man, but the horse, which had disappeared in this unaccountable manner. It seemed improbable that two living substances of such bulk should pass out of being and leave no trace behind them. They must literally have melted into thin air.

No, they hadn't. At least the black mare hadn't, for she was discovered by several members of the searching-party a little before noon. When found, she was quietly cropping the damp herbage at the edge of the cranberry swamp at the rear of Squire Harrington's farm. She was wholly uninjured, and had evidently spent the night there. The bit had been removed from her mouth, but the bridle hung intact round her neck. The saddle, however, like its owner, had disappeared from her back.

Then the men began a systematic search in the interior of the swamp. They soon came upon the saddle, which had apparently been deliberately unbuckled, removed from off the mare, and deposited on a dry patch of ground, near the edge of the morass. A little further in the interior they came upon a man's coat, made of dark brown stuff. This garment was identified by one of the party as belong to Savareen. It was wet and besmirched with mud, and, in fact was lying half in and half out of a little puddle of water when it was found. Then the searchers made sure of finding the body.

But in this they were disappointed. They explored the recesses of the swamp from end to end and side to side with the utmost thoroughness, but found nothing further to reward their search. The ground was too soft and marshy to retain any traces of footsteps, and the mare and saddle furnished the only evidence that the object of their quest had been in the neighborhood of the swamp--and of course this evidence was of the most vague and inconclusive character.

Then the party proceeded in a body to the missing man's house. Here another surprise awaited them. The coat was at once recognised by Mrs. Savareen as belonging to her husband, but IT WAS NOT THE COAT WORN BY HIM AT THE TIME OF HIS DISAPPEARANCE. Of this there was no doubt whatever. In fact, he had not worn it for more than a week previously. His wife distinctly remembered having folded and laid it away in the top of a large trunk on the Saturday of the week before last, since which time she had never set eyes on it. Here was a deepening of the mystery.

The search was kept up without intermission for several days, nearly all of the farmers in the vicinity taking part in it, even to the neglect of the harvest work which demanded their attention. Squire Harrington was especially active, and left no stone unturned to unravel the mystery. Lapierre gave up all his time to the search, and left the Royal Oak to the care of its landlady. The local constabulary bestirred themselves as they had never done before. Every place, likely and un-likely, where a man's body might possibly lie concealed; every tract of bush and woodland; every barn and out building; every hollow and ditch; every field and fence corner, was explored with careful minuteness. Even the wells of the district were peered into and examined for traces of the thirteen stone of humanity which had so unaccountably disappeared from off the face of the earth. Doctor Scott, the local coroner, held himself in readiness to summon a coroner's jury at the shortest notice. When all these measures proved unavailing, a public meeting of the inhabit-ants was convened, and funds were subscribed to still further prosecute the search. A reward of a hundred pounds was offered for any information which should lead to the discovery of the missing man, dead or alive, or, which should throw any light upon his fate. Hand-bills proclaiming this reward, and describing the man's personal appearance, were exhibited in every bar room and other conspicuous place throughout Westchester and the adjacent townships. Advertisements, setting forth the main facts, were inserted in the principal newspapers of Toronto, Hamilton and London, as well as in those of several of the nearest county towns.

All to no purpose. Days--weeks--months passed by, and furnished not the shadow of a clue to the mysterious disappearance of Reginald Bourchier Savareen on the night of Monday, the 17th of July, 1854.

CHAPTER VI.
SPECULATIONS.

For a long time subsequent to the night of the disappearance a more puzzled community than the one settled along the Millbrook and Spotswood road would have been hard to find in Upper Canada. At first sight it seemed probable that the missing man had been murdered for his money. On the afternoon of the day when he was last seen in Millbrook the fact of his having four hundred pounds in bank bills in his possession was known to a great many people, for, as already intimated, he told the story of his dispute at the bank to pretty nearly everyone with whom he came in contact during the subsequent portion of the day, and he in every instance wound up his narration by proclaiming to all whom it might concern that he had the notes in his pocket. But it was difficult to fix upon any particular individual as being open to suspicion. There had been no attempt on the part of any of his associates on that afternoon to detain him in town, and his remaining there until the evening had been entirely due to his own inclinations. So far as was known, he had not been followed by any person after his departure from the Peacock at 7.45. Anyone following would have had no prospect of overtaking him unless mounted on a good horse, and must perforce have passed through the toll-gate. According to the testimony of Perry and his wife, nobody had passed through the gate in his wake, nor for more than an hour after him. But--mystery of mysteries--where had he managed to hide himself and his mare during the two or three minutes which had elapsed between his departure from the gate and the arrival there of Lapierre? And, if he had been murdered, what had become of his body?

Had it been at all within the bounds of reason to suspect Stolliver, suspicion would certainly have fallen upon that personage. But any idea of the kind was altogether out of the question. Stolliver was a boorish, uncompanionable fellow, but a more unlikely man to commit such a serious crime could not have been found in the whole country side. Again, he could not have had any conceivable motive for making away with Savareen, as he had been working all day in the fields and knew nothing about the four hundred pounds. Besides, a little quiet investigation proved the thing to be an absolute impossibility. At the time of Savareen's disappearance, Stolliver had been sitting at his own table, in the company of his wife, his family, and a grown-up female servant. He had sat down to table at about a quarter to eight, and had not risen therefrom until several minutes after the town bell had ceased to ring. On rising, he had gone out with his two boys--lads of thirteen and fifteen years of age respectively--and had barely taken up a position with them on the front fence when Lapierre came along and questioned him, as related in a former chapter. So it was certainly not worth while to pursue that branch of enquiry any farther.

The only other persons upon whom the shadow of suspicion could by any possibility fall were Lapierre and Jonathan Perry. Well, so far as the latter was concerned the idea was too absurd for serious consideration. To begin with, Jonathan was seventy-six years of age, feeble and almost decrepid. Then, he was a man of excellent character, and, notwithstanding his humble station in life, was liked and respected by all who knew him. Finally, he could not have done away with Savareen without the knowledge and concurrence of his wife, a gentle, kindly old soul, who found her best consolation between the covers of her bible, and who would not have raised her finger against a worm. So that branch of the enquiry might also be considered as closed.

As to Lapierre, the idea was at least as preposterous as either of the others. The jovial landlord of the Royal Oak was on the whole about as likely a man to commit robbery or murder as the bishop of the diocese. He was of a cheery, open nature; was not greedy or grasping; had a fairly prosperous business, and was tolerably well-to-do. On the night of the 17th, he had undertaken to go down town and bring home the absent man, but he had done so at the pressing request of the man's wife, and out of pure kindness of heart. When setting out on his mission he knew nothing about the altercation at the bank, and was consequently ignorant that Savareen had any considerable sum of money on his person. His first knowledge on these subjects had been communicated to him by Perry, and before that time the man had disappeared. It also counted for something that Savareen and he had always been on the most friendly terms, and that Savareen was one of his best customers. But, even if he had been the most bloodthirsty of mankind, he had positively had no time to perpetrate a murder. The two or three minutes elapsing between Savareen's departure from the toll-gate and Lapierre's arrival there had been too brief to admit of the latter's having meanwhile killed the former and made away with his body; to say nothing of his having also made such a disposition of the black mare as to enable it to be found in Cranberry Swamp on the following day.

After a while people began to ask whether it was probable that any murder at all had been committed. The finding of the coat was an unfathomable mystery, but it really furnished no evidence one way or the other. And if there had been a murder, how was it that no traces of the body were discoverable? How was it that no cry or exclamation of any kind had been heard by old Jonathan, sitting there at the door in the open air on a still night? It was certain that his ears had been wide open, and ready enough to take in whatever was stirring, for he had heard the sound of Count Frontenac's hoofs as they came clattering down the road.

Such questions as these were constantly in the mouths of the people of that neighborhood for some days after the disappearance, but they met with no satisfactory answer from any quarter, and as the time passed by it began to be believed that no light would ever be thrown upon the most mysterious occurrence that had ever taken place since that part of the country had been first settled. One of the constables, discouraged by repeated failures, ventured in all seriousness to express a suspicion that Savareen had been bodily devoured by his mare. How else could you account for no trace of him being visible anywhere?

By an unaccountable oversight, Shuttleworth had kept no memorandum of the number of the notes paid over to Savareen, and it was thus impossible to trace them.

CHAPTER VII.
"A WIDOW, HUSBANDLESS, SUBJECT TO FEARS."

The position of the missing man's wife was a particularly trying and painful one--a position imperatively calling for the sympathy of the community in which she lived. That sympathy was freely accorded to her, but time alone could bring any thing like tranquillity to a mind harrassed by such manifold anxieties as hers. After a lapse of a few weeks Squire Harrington generously offered to take the farm off her hands, but to this proposal she was for some time loath to assent. In spite of her fears and misgivings, fitful gleams of hope that her husband would return to her flitted across her mind. If he came back he should find her at her post. Meanwhile the neighbors showed her much kindness. They voluntarily formed an organisation of labor, and harvested her crops, threshed them out and conveyed them to market for her. Her brother, a young man of eighteen, came out from town and took up his abode with her, so that she would not be left wholly desolate among strangers. And so the summer and autumn glided by.

But this state of things could not last. The strange solitude of her destiny preyed sorely upon her and when the first snows of winter arrived, bringing with them no tidings of the absent one, the fortitude of the bereaved woman broke down. She gave up the farm, and with her little baby boy and such of her household belongings as she chose to retain, went back to the home of her parents in Millbrook. She was a few hundred dollars better off in this world's goods than she had been when she had left that home about thirteen months before, but her spirit was sadly bent, if not altogether broken, and the brightness seemed to have utterly faded out of her life.

In process of time she became in some degree accustomed, if not reconciled to her lot. But her situation was, to say the least, anomalous. Her parents were, on the whole, kind and considerate, but she was conscious of being, after a fashion, isolated from them and from all the rest of the world. She felt, as one who was, in the language of the proverb, neither maid, wife nor widow. She knew not whether her child's father was living or dead. She was barely twenty-three years of age, but she was not free to form a second marriage, even if she had had any inclination for such a union, which, to do her justice, she had not, for she cherished the memory of her absent lord with fond affection, and persisted in believing that, even if he were living, it was through no fault of his own that he remained away from her. She lived a very quiet and secluded life. In spite of her mother's importunities, she seldom stirred out of doors on week days, and saw few visitors. She was a regular attendant at church on Sundays, and sought to find relief from mental depression in the consolations of religion. Her chief consolation, however, lay in her child, upon whom she lavished all the tenderness of a soft and gentle nature. She fondly sought to trace in the little fellow's bright features some resemblance to the lineaments of him she had loved and lost. To do this successfully required a rather strong effort of the imagination, for, to tell the truth, the boy favored his mother's side of the house, and was no more like his father than he was like the twelve patriarchs. But a fond mother often lives in an ideal world of her own creation, and can trace resemblances invisible to ordinary mortals. So it was with this mother, who often declared that her boy had a way of "looking out of his eyes," as she expressed it, which forcibly brought back the memory of happy days which had forever passed away.

Of course Savareen's relatives in the old country received due notice of his strange disappearance, and of the various circumstances connected with that event. Mrs. Savareen had herself communicated the facts, and had also sent over a copy of the Millbrook **Sentinel**, containing a long and minute account of the affair. A letter arrived from Herefordshire in due course, acknowledging the receipt of these missives, and enquiring whether the lost had been found. Several communications passed to and fro during the first few months, after which, as there was really nothing further to write about, the correspondence fell off; it being of course understood that should any new facts turn up, they should be promptly made known.

The stars do not pause in their spheres to take note of the afflictions of us mortals here below. To the bereaved woman it seemed unaccountable that the succeeding months should come and go as formerly, and as though nothing had occurred to take the saltness and savor out of her young life. Ever and anon her slumbers were disturbed by weird dreams, in which the lost one was presented before her in all sorts of frightful situations. In these dreams which came to her in the silent watches of the night, she never seemed to look upon her husband as dead. He always seemed to be living, but surrounded by inextricable complications involving great trouble and danger. She sometimes awoke from these night visions with a loud cry which startled the household, and proved how greatly her nerves had been shaken by the untoward circumstances of her fate.

In the early spring of the ensuing year she sustained another painful bereavement through the death of her mother. This event imparted an additional element of sadness to her already cloudy existence; but it was not without certain attendant compensations, as it rendered necessary a more active course of life on her part, and so left her less time to brood over her earlier sorrow. No Benvolio was needed to tell us that

> "One fire burns out another's burning:
> One pain is lessened by another's anguish."

Most of us have at one time or another been forced to learn that hard truth for ourselves. This forlorn woman had probably never read the passage, but her experience brought abundant confirmation of it home to her at this time. She was driven to assume the internal management of the household, and found grateful solace in the occupations which the position involved. She once more began to take an interest in the prosaic affairs of everyday life, and became less addicted to looking forward to a solitary, joyless old age. So that, all things considered, this second bereavement was not to be regarded in the light of an affliction absolutely without mitigation.

It might well have been supposed that the place she was now called upon to fill would have been the means of drawing closer the ties between her surviving parent and herself. For a time it certainly had that effect. Her presence in his house must have done much to soften the blow to her father, and her practical usefulness was made manifest every hour of the day. She carefully ministered to his domestic needs, and did what she could to alleviate the burden which had been laid upon him. But the old, old story was once more repeated. In little more than a year from the time her mother had been laid in her grave, she was made aware of the fact that the household was to receive a new mistress. In other words, she was to be introduced to a stepmother. The event followed hard upon the announcement. As a necessary consequence she was compelled to assume a secondary place in her father's house.

It may be true that first marriages are sometimes made in Heaven. It is even possible that second marriages may now and then be forged in the same workshop. But it was soon brought home to Mrs. Savareen that this particular marriage was not among the number. Her stepmother, who was not much older than herself, proved a veritable thorn in her side. She was made to perceive that she and her little boy were regarded in the light of encumbrances, to be tolerated until they could be got rid of. But not passively tolerated. The stepmother was a rather coarse-grained piece of clay--an unsympathetic, unfeeling woman, who knew how to say and to do unpleasant things without any apparent temper or ill-will. The immortal clockmaker, when he was in a more quaintly sententious humor than common, once propounded the doctrine that the direct road to a mother's heart is through her child. He might have added the equally incontestable proposition that the most effectual method of torturing a mother's heart is through the same medium. The mother who has an only child, who is all the world to her, is actually susceptible to anything in the shape of interference with her maternal prerogatives. Such interference, by whomsoever exercised, is wholly intolerable to her. This susceptibility may perhaps be a feminine weakness, but it is a veritable maternal instinct, and one with which few who have observed it will have the heart to find fault. In Mrs. Savareen's bosom this foible existed in a high state of development, and her stepmother so played upon it as to make life under the same roof with her a cross too hard to be borne. After a few months' trial, the younger of the two women resolved that a new home must be found for herself and her little boy. The carrying out of this resolve rendered some consideration necessary, for her own unaided means were inadequate for her support. Her father, though not what could be called a poor man, was far from rich, and he had neither the means nor the will to maintain two establishments, however humble. But she was expert with her needle, and did not despair of being able to provide for the slender wants of herself and child. She rented and furnished a small house in the town, where she found that there was no ground for present anxiety as to her livelihood. There was plenty of needlework to be had to keep her nimble fingers busy from morn till night, and her income from the first was in excess of her expenditure. She was constrained to lead a humdrum sort of existence, but it was brightened by the presence and companionship of her boy, who was a constant source of pride and delight to her. Whenever she caught herself indulging in a despondent mood, she took herself severely to task for repining at a lot which might have lacked this element of brightness, and which lacking that, would, it seemed to her, have been too dreary for human endurance.

No useful purpose would be served by lingering over this portion of the narrative. Suffice it to say that the current of the lonely woman's life flowed smoothly on several years, during which she received no tidings of her lost husband and heard nothing to throw the faintest scintilla of light upon his mysterious disappearance. Little Reginald grew apace, and continued to be the one consolation in her great bereavement--the solitary joy which reconciled her to her environment.

CHAPTER VIII.
A GUEST ARRIVES AT THE ROYAL OAK.

It was getting on towards the middle of the month of August, 1859. The harvest all along the Millbrook and Spotswood road was in full progress. And a bounteous harvest it was, even for that favored region. Squire Harrington confidently counted upon a yield of fifty bushels of wheat to the acre. True, he was a model farmer, and knew how to make the most of a good season, but his neighbors were not far behind him, and were looking forward to full granaries when threshing should be over. For once there was little or no grumbling at the dispensations of Providence. The weather had been as propitious as though the local tillers of the soil had themselves had a voice in the making of it, and even gruff Mark Stolliver was constrained to admit that there were fewer grounds for remonstrating with the Great Disposer of events than usual at this season of the year. Every wheat field in the township presented an active spectacle throughout the day. The cradles were busily plied from early morn till nightfall, and the swaths of golden grain furnished heavy work for the rakers and binders. The commercial crisis of 1857 had made itself felt in the district, as well as in all other parts of Upper Canada. Many of the farmers had fallen considerably behindhand, and had for once in a way felt the grip of hard times. But the prolific crops which were now being gathered in bade fair to extricate them from such obligations as they had been compelled to incur, and the prevailing tone was one of subdued though heartfelt satisfaction.

On the evening of Saturday, the 13th of the month, sundry of the yeomen who lived thereabouts assembled at Lapierre's, after a hard week's work, to congratulate one another on the prospects of the harvest, and to discuss a few tankards of the reaming ale for which the Royal Oak was famous throughout the township. The landlord himself was on hand as usual, to dispense the hospitalities of his bar and larder. The five years which had rolled over his head since that memorable night of Savareen's disappearance had left but slight traces of their passage upon his jovial countenance. He had never been able to fathom the impenetrable secret of that strange July night, but he had all along been wont to remark that the mystery would be cleared up some day, and that he confidently expected to hear some tidings of the missing man before he died. As for his guests, though most of them had resided in the neighborhood at the time of his disappearance, they had long ceased to give themselves any particular concern about the matter. So long as there had seemed to be any prospect of getting at the bottom of the affair they had taken a vigorous part in the search, and had exerted themselves to bring the mystery to light; but when month succeeded month without supplying any clue to the puzzle, they had gradually resigned themselves to the situation, and, except when the topic came up for discussion at their Saturday night meetings, they seldom indulged in anything more than a passing allusion to it.

Ten o'clock had struck, and it seemed improbable that any further company would arrive. The assembled guests, to the number of seven or eight, sat in their accustomed places around a goodly-sized table in the room behind the bar. Lapierre occupied an easy chair, placed near the door communicating with the bar, so as to be handy in case of his being needed there. Farmer Donaldson had just regaled the circle with his favorite ditty, The Roast Beef of Old England, which he flattered himself he could render with fine effect. Having concluded his performance, he sat modestly back in his elbow-chair, and bowed to the vociferous plaudits accorded to him. The tankards were then charged afresh, and each man devoted himself to the allaying of his thirst for the next minute or two. Mine host had promised to give Faintly as Tolls the Evening Chime in the course of the evening, and was now called upon to redeem his pledge.

"Ah," he remarked, "that vas alvays a faforite song of mine. And ton't you remember how font of it our frient Safareen used to pe? He used to call for it regular efery Saturday night, schoost pefore supper in the old times. Ah, put that wass a strange peesiness. I haf never peen aple to think of it without perspiring." And so saying, he dived into the pocket of his white linen jacket, and produced therefrom a red silk handkerchief, with which he mopped his beaming countenance until it shone again.

"Ay," responded Farmer Donaldson, "that was the strangest thing as ever happened in these parts. I wonder if it will ever be cleared up."

"You know my opinion apout that," resumed the host, "I alvays said he vould turn up. But it is--let me see--yes, it is more that fife years ago. It wass on the night of the sefenteenth of Chooly, 1854; and here it is, the mittle of Aucust, 1859. Vell, vell, how the years go py! Safareen was a coot sort. I thought much of him, and woot like to see him once acain."

"I don't say but what he was a good fellow," remarked one of the company; "but I can tell you he had a devil of a temper of his own when his blood was up. I remember one night in this very room when he had some words with Sam Dolsen about that black mare o' his'n. He fired up like a tiger, and that scar on his cheek glowed like a carbuncle. It seemed as if it was going to crack open. I made sure he was going to drop into Sam, and he would 'a done, too, if our landlord hadn't interfered and calmed him down."

"Yes, yes," interrupted Farmer Donaldson; "Savareen had his tempers, no doubt, when he had been drinking more free than common; but he was a jolly feller, all the same. I wish he was with us at this moment."

This sentiment was pretty generally re-echoed all round the festive board. Just then a rather heavy footstep was heard to enter the adjoining bar-room from out-side. The landlord rose and passed out through the doorway, to see if his services were required. The door of communication was left open behind him, so that the company in the inner room had no difficulty in seeing and hearing everything that took place.

In the middle of the bar room stood a short heavy-set man, whose dress and bearing pronounced him to be a stranger in those parts. He was apparently middle-aged--say somewhere between thirty-five and forty. His clothing was of expensive material, but cut after a style more *prononce* than was then seen in Canada, or has ever since been much in vogue here. His hat was a broad-brimmed Panama, which cost twenty dollars if it cost a penny. His coat, so far as could be seen under his thin summer duster--was of fine bluish cloth, short of waist, long of skirt, and--the duster notwithstanding--plentifully besprinkled and travel-stained with dust. The waistcoat, which seemed to be of the same material as the coat, was very open-breasted, and displayed a considerable array of shirt front. Across the left side was hung a heavy gold watch-chain, from which depended two great bulbous-looking seals. On his feet he wore a pair of gaiters of patent leather, white from the dust of the road. In one hand he carried a light, jaunty Malacca cane, while the other grasped a Russian-leather portmanteau, called by him and by persons of his kind a valise. He wore no gloves--a fact which enabled you to see on the middle finger of his left hand a huge cluster diamond ring, worth any price from a thousand dol-lars upwards. His face was closely shaven, except for a prominent moustache. He had crisp, curling black hair, worn tolerably short. His eyes were rather dull and vacant, not because he was either slow or stupid, but because he felt or affected to feel, a sublime indifference to all things sublunary. You would have taken him for a man who had run the gauntlet of all human experiences--a man to whom noth-ing presented itself in the light of a novelty, and who disdained to appear much interested in anything you might say or do. Taken altogether he had that foreign or rather cosmopolitan look characteristic of the citizen of the United States who has led an unsettled, wandering life. His aspect was fully borne out by his accent, when he began to speak.

"Air you the landlord?" he asked, as the host stepped forward to greet him.

He received a reply in the affirmative.

"This, then, is the Royal Oak tavern, and your name is Lapierre?"

Two nods signified the host's further assent to these undeniable propositions.

"Have you got a spare bedroom, and can you put me up from now till Monday morning?"

The landlord again signified his assent, whereupon the stranger put down his cane and portmanteau on a bench and proceeded to divest himself of his wrapper.

"You haf had supper?" asked Lapierre.

"Well, I had a light tea down to Millbrook, but I know your Saturday night customs at the Royal Oak, and if you hain't got any objections I'd like to take a hand in your eleven o'clock supper. To tell the truth, I'm sharp-set, and I know you always have a bite of something appetizing about that time."

Upon being informed that supper would be ready at the usual hour, and that he would be welcome to a seat at the board, he signified a desire to be shown to his room, so that he could wash and make himself presentable. In response to an enquiry about his horse, he intimated that that animal for the present consisted of Shank's mare; that he had ridden up from town with Squire Harrington, and dismounted at that gentleman's gate. "The Squire offered to drive me on as far as here," he added; "but as it was only a short walk I reckoned I'd come on afoot."

Without further parley the guest was shown to his chamber, whence he emerged a few minutes later, and presented himself before the company assembled in the room behind the bar.

"Hope I ain't intruding, gentlemen," he remarked, as he took a vacant seat at the lower end of the table; "I've often heard of the good times you have here on Saturday nights. Heard of 'em when I was a good many hundred miles from here, and when I didn't expect ever to have the pleasure of joining your mess. Guess I'd better introduce myself. My name's Thomas Jefferson Haskins. I live at Nashville, Tennessee, where I keep a hotel and do a little in horseflesh now an' agin. Now, I shall take it as a favor if you'll allow the landlord to re-fill your glasses at my expense, and then drink good-luck to my expedition." All this with much volubility, and without a trace of bashfulness.

The company all round the table signified their hearty acquiescence, and while the landlord was replenishing the tankards, the stranger proceeded to further enlighten them respecting his personal affairs. He informed them that a man had cleared out from Nashville about six months ago, leaving him, the speaker, in the lurch to the tune of twenty-seven hundred dollars. A few days since he had learned that the fugitive had taken up his quarters at Spotswood, in Upper Canada, and he had accordingly set out for that place with intent to obtain a settlement. He had reached Millbrook by the seven o'clock express this evening, only to find that he was still fifteen miles from his destination. Upon inquiry, he learned that the stage from Millbrook for Spotswood ran only once a day, leaving Millbrook at seven o'clock in the morning. There would not be another stage until Monday morning. He was on the point of hiring a special conveyance, and of driving through that night, when all of a sudden he had remembered that Lapierre's tavern was on the Millbrook and Spotswood road, and only three miles away. He had long ago heard such accounts of the Royal Oak and its landlord, and particularly of the Saturday night suppers, that he had resolved to repair thither and remain over for Monday's stage. "I was going to hire a livery to bring me out here," he added, "but a gentleman named Squire Harrington, who heard me give the order for the buggy, told me he lived close by the Royal Oak, and that I was welcome to ride out with him, as he was just going to start for home. That saved me a couple of dollars. And so, here I be."

Lapierre could not feel otherwise than highly flattered by the way the stranger referred to his establishment, but he was wholly at a loss to understand how the fame of the Royal Oak, and more especially of the Saturday night suppers, had extended to so great a distance as Nashville. In response to his inquiries on these points, however, Mr. Thomas Jefferson Haskins gave a clear and lucid explanation, which will be found in the next chapter.

CHAPTER IX.
THE GUEST CREATES A SENSATION
AT THE ROYAL OAK.

"Well," said Haskins, "I didn't hear of you quite so far off as Nashville. It was when I was travelling in Kentucky buying horses, last year. At Lexington I fell in with an English chap named Randall, who used to live in this neighborhood. I hired him to buy horses for me. He was with me about three months, an' if I could only 'a' kept him sober he'd been with me yet, for he was about as keen a judge of a horse as ever I came across in my born days, and knew mighty well how to make a bargain. Well, we hadn't been together a week afore he begun to tell me about a place where he used to live in Canada West, where he said a little money went a long way, and where good horses could be bought cheap. He wanted me to send him up here to buy for me, and I don't know but I should 'a' done it if I'd found he was to be trusted. But he would drink like all creation when he had money. Old Bourbon was a thing he couldn't resist. He had an awful poor opinion of all the rest of our American institootions, and used to say they wa'n't o' no account as compared to what he used to have to home in England; but when it come to Bourbon whisky, he was as full-mouthed as Uncle Henry Clay himself. He 'lowed there wa'n't anything either in England or in Canada to touch it. An' when he got four or five inches of it inside him, there was no gittin' along with him nohow. There wa'n't anything on airth he wouldn't do to git a couple of inches more, and when he got them he was the catawamptiousest critter I ever did see. You couldn't place any more dependence on him than on a free nigger. Besides, he used to neglect his wife, and a man who neglects his wife ain't a man to trust with a couple o' thousand dollars at a time. No sir-ree! Not much, he ain't. But, as I was sayin', the way he used to harp on this place o' Lapierre's was a caution. Whenever we used to git planted down in one of our cross-road taverns, he'd turn up his nose till you could see clean down his throat into his stommick. The fact is, our country taverns ain't up to much, an' sometimes I could hardly stand 'em myself. When we'd come in after a hard day's ridin', and git sot down to a feed of heavy short-cake and fat pork, then Randall 'ud begin to blow about the grub up here at Lapierre's. He used to tell about the hot suppers served up here to a passel o' farmers on Saturday nights till I most got sick o' hearing him. But I see your mugs air empty again, gentlemen. Landlord, please to do your dooty, and score it up to yours truly."

During this long harangue the assembled guests alternately scanned the speaker and each other with inquiring but vacant countenances. They were puzzling themselves to think who this Randall could be, as no man of that name had ever been known in that community. When Mr. Haskins paused in his discourse, and gave his order for replenishment, Farmer Donaldson was about to remonstrate against this second treat at the expense of a stranger, and to propose that he himself should stand sponsor for the incoming refreshments. But before he could get out a word, the landlord suddenly sprang from his seat with a white, agitated face.

"Tell me," he said, addressing the stranger--"What like is this Rantall? Please to tescripe his features."

"Well," drawled the person addressed, after a short pause--"there ain't much to describe about him. He's a tallish feller--fully four inches taller'n I be. He's broad and stout--a big man ginerally. Weighs, I should say, not much under a hundred and ninety. Ruther light complected, and has a long cut in his face that shows aw-ful white when he gits his back up. Thunder! he pretty nearly scared me with that gash one night when he was drunk. It seemed to open and shut like a clam-shell, and made him look like a Voodoo priest! You'd think the blood was goan to spurt out by the yard."

By this time every pair of eyes in the room was staring into the speaker's face with an expression of bewildered astonishment. Not a man there but recognized the description as a vivid, if somewhat exaggerated portraiture of the long-lost Reginald Bourchier Savareen.

The stranger from Tennessee readily perceived that he had produced a genuine sensation. He gazed from one to another for a full minute without speaking. Then he gave vent to his surcharged feelings by the exclamation: "For the land's sake!"

An air of speechless bewilderment still pervaded the entire group. They sat silent as statues, without motion, and almost without breath.

Lapierre was the first to recover himself. By a significant gesture he imposed continued silence upon the company, and began to ask questions. He succeeded in eliciting some further pertinent information.

Haskins was unable to say when Randall had acquired a familiarity with the ways and doings of the people residing in the vicinity of the Royal Oak, but it must have been some time ago, as he had lived in the States long enough to have become acquainted with various localities there. As to when and why he had left Canada the stranger was also totally ignorant. He knew, however, that Randall was living in the city of New York about three months ago, as he had seen him there, and had visited him at his lodgings on Amity street in May, when he (Haskins) had attended as a delegate to a sporting convention. At that time Randall had been employed in some capacity in Hitchcock's sale stable, and made a few dollars now and again by breeding dogs. He lived a needy hand-to-mouth existence, and his poor wife had a hard time of it. His drinking habits prevented him from getting ahead in the world, and he never staid long in one place, but the speaker had no doubt that he might still be heard of at Hitchcock's by anybody who wanted to hunt him up. "But," added Mr. Haskins, "I hope I haven't got him into trouble by coming here to-night. Has he done anything? Anything criminal, I mean?"

After a moment's deliberation, Lapierre told the whole story. There was no doubt in the mind of any member of the company that Randall and Savareen were "parts of one stupendous whole." The one important question for consideration was: What use ought to be made of the facts thus strangely brought to light?

By this time supper was announced, and the stranger's news, exciting as it was, did not prevent the guests from doing ample justice to it. Haskins was loud in his praises of the "spread," as he termed it. "Jack Randall," he remarked, "could lie when he had a mind to, but he told the holy truth when he bragged you up as far ahead of the Kentucky cooks. Yes, I don't mind if I do take another mossel of that frickersee. Dog me if it don't beat canvas-backs."

Before the meeting broke up it was agreed on all hands that for the present it would be advisable for the guests to allow the morrow to pass before saying anything to their wives or anyone else about Mr. Haskins' disclosures. It was further resolved that that gentleman should accompany Lapierre to Millbrook after breakfast in the morning, and that Mrs. Savareen's father should be made acquainted with the known facts. It was just possible, after all, that Jack Randall might be Jack Randall, and not Savareen, in which case it was desirable to save the lost man's wife from cruel agitation to no purpose. It would be for her father, after learning all that they knew, to communicate the facts to her or to withhold them, as might seem best to him. On this understanding the company broke up on the stroke of midnight. I am by no means prepared to maintain that their pledges were in all cases kept, and that they each and every one went to sleep without taking their wives into confidence respecting the strange disclosures of the night.

CHAPTER X.
NO. 77 AMITY STREET.

The next day was Sunday, but this circumstance did not deter Lapierre from hitching up his horse and conveying his guest down to Millbrook at an early hour. The pair called at the house of Mrs. Savareen's father before ten o'clock, and had a long interview with him. Church services began at eleven, but it was remarked by the Methodist congregation, and commented upon as a thing almost without precedent, that Mrs. Savareen and her father were both absent on that day.

The old gentleman was much disturbed by what he heard from Mr. Haskins. His daughter had passed through an ordeal of great suffering, and had finally become reconciled to her lot. To tell her this news would be to open the old wounds afresh, and to bring back the domestic grief which time had about dispelled. Yet his course seemed clear. To tell her the truth was an imperative duty. It would be shameful to permit her to go on mourning for one who was in every way unworthy, and who might turn up at any unexpected moment to the destruction of her peace of mind. Moreover, the secret was already known to too many persons to admit of any hope that it would be permanently kept. She must be told, and there could be no question that her father was the proper person to tell her. She would, however, wish to personally see and converse with the man who had brought the news, so there was no time to be lost. Leaving his two visitors to await his return, the old man set out with a sad heart for his daughter's house. He found her and her little boy just ready to set out for church, but the first glance at her father's face told her that something had happened, and that there would be no church-going for that day. She sat pale and trembling as she listened, and the old man himself was not much more composed. He broke the news as gently as he could, and she bore it better than he had expected, suppressing her agitation and taking in all the details without interruption. Even when all the circumstances had been laid before her, her self-command did not desert her. Yes, she must see the stranger from Tennessee. Possibly she might extract something from him which others had failed to elicit. Her father accordingly went back to his own home, and brought Mr. Haskins over. The three spent several hours in talking of the affair, but the stranger had nothing more to tell, and finally took his leave, promising to call on his way back from Spotswood.

Father and daughter spent the evening together, and tried to reach some definite conclusion as to what, if anything, ought to be done. There could be no reasonable doubt that Randall and Savareen were one. Since there was just the shadow of doubt, and the want of absolute certainty, made it impossible for Mrs. Savareen to leave the matter as it stood. She felt that she must know the whole truth.

A course was finally decided upon. Father and daughter would start for New York without delay and probe the matter to the bottom. The news could not wholly be kept from the stepmother, but she was enjoined to maintain a strict silence on the subject until further light should be thrown upon it. Master Reginald was temporarily left in her charge.

They started for New York by the mid-day express on Monday, and reached their destination on Tuesday afternoon. Lodgings were secured at a quiet, respectable hotel, and then the old man set out alone to hunt up Hitchcock's stable. He had no difficulty in finding it, and the man in charge of the office readily gave him the information he sought. Jack Randall was no longer employed at the establishment, but he lodged with his wife at No. 77 Amity street. The best time to catch him at home was early in the morning. He was of a convivial turn, and generally spent his evenings about town. He was supposed to be pretty hard up, but that was his chronic condition, and, so far as known, he was not in absolute want. With these tidings the father returned to his daughter.

Mrs. Savareen could not bear the idea of permitting the evening to pass without some further effort. She determined to pay a visit to 77 Amity street, in person, and if possible to see the man's wife for herself. A servant-maid in the hotel undertook to pilot her to her destination, which was but a short distance away. It was about eight o'clock when she set out and the light of day was fast disappearing. Upon reaching the corner of Amity street and Broadway, she dismissed her attendant and made the rest of the journey alone. The numbers on the doors of the houses were a sufficient direction for her, and she soon found herself ringing at the bell of 77.

Her summons was answered by a seedy-looking porter. Yes, Mrs. Randall was upstairs in her room on the third story. Mr. Randall was out. The lady could easily find the way for herself. Second door to the left on the third flat. Straight up. And so saying the man disappeared into the darkness at the rear of the house, leaving the visitor to group her way up two dimly-lighted stairways as best she could.

The place was evidently a lodging-house of very inferior description to be so near the palatial temples of commerce just round the corner. The halls were uncarpeted, and, indeed, without the least sign of furniture of any sort. As Mrs. Savareen slowly ascended one flight of stairs after another, she began to wonder if she had not done an unwise thing in venturing alone into a house and locality of which she knew nothing. Having reached the third story she found herself in total darkness, except for such faint twilight as found its way through a back window. This however was just sufficient to enable her to perceive the second door on the left. She advanced towards it and knocked. A female voice responded by an invitation to enter. She quietly turned the knob of the door and advanced into the room.

CHAPTER XI.
AN INTERVIEW BY CANDLELIGHT.

The apartment in which the "bold discoverer in an unknown sea" found herself presented an appearance far from cheerful or attractive. It was of small dimensions, but too large for the meagre supply of furniture it contained. The unpapered walls displayed a monotonous surface of bare whitewash in urgent need of renewal. In one corner was an impoverished looking bed, on which reposed an infant of a few months old. At the foot of the bed was a cheap toilet stand, with its accessories. In the adjacent corner was a door apparently opening into a closet or inner receptacle of some kind, against which was placed a battered leather trunk with a broken hasp. A small table of stained pine, without any covering, stood near the middle of the room, and two or three common wooden chairs were distributed here and there against the walls. The faint light of expiring day found admission by means of a window looking out upon the roofs to the rear of the house. The only artificial light consisted of a solitary candle placed on the table, at the far end of which sat a woman engaged in sewing.

The light, dim and ineffectual as it was, served to show that this woman was in a state of health which her friends, if she had any, must have deemed to be anything but satisfactory. It was easy to perceive that she had once possessed an attractive and rather pretty face. Some portion of her attractiveness still remained, but the beauty had been washed away by privation and misery, leaving behind nothing but a faint simulacrum of its former self. She was thin and fragile to the point of emaciation, insomuch that her print dress hung upon her as loosely as a morning wrapper. Her cheeks were sunken and hollow, and two dark patches beneath a pair of large blue eyes plainly indicated serious nervous waste. In addition to these manifest signs of a low state of bodily health, her pinched features had a worn, weary expression which told a sad tale of long and continuous suffering. Most of these things her visitor, with feminine quickness of perception, took in at the first momentary glance, and any pre-conceived feeling of hostility which may have had a place in her heart gave way to a sentiment of womanly sympathy. Clearly enough, any display of jealous anger would be wholly out of place in such a presence and situation.

Mrs. Savareen had not given much pre-consideration as to her line of action during the impending interview. She had merely resolved to be guided by circumstances, and what she saw before her made her errand one of some difficulty. Her main object, of course, was to ascertain, beyond the possibility of doubt, whether the man calling himself Jack Randall was the man known to her as Reginald Bourchier Savareen.

The tenant of the room rose as her visitor entered, and even that slight exertion brought on a hollow cough which was pitiful to hear.

"I am sorry to see," gently remarked the visitor, "that you are far from well."

"Yes," was the reply; "I've got a cold, and ain't very smart. Take a chair." And so saying, she placed a chair in position, and made a not ungraceful motion towards it with her hand.

Mrs. Savareen sat down, and began to think what she would say next. Her hostess saved her from much thought on the matter by enquiring whether she had called to see Mr. Randall.

"Yes," replied Mrs. Savareen, "I would like to see him for a few moments, if convenient."

"Well, *I* am sorry he's out, and I don't suppose he'll be in for some time. He's generally out in the fore part of the evening; but he's most always home in the morning. Is it anything I can tell him?"

Here was a nice complication. Had Mrs. Savareen been a student of Moliere, the fitting reply to such a question under such circumstances would doubtless have risen to her lips. But I shrewdly suspect that she had never heard of the famous Frenchman, whose works were probably an unknown quantity in Millbrook in those days. After a momentary hesitation she fenced with the question, and put one in her turn.

"Do you know if he has heard from his friends in Hertfordshire lately?"

"Hertfordshire? O, that is the place he comes from in the Old Country. No, he never hears from there. I have often wanted him to write to his friends in England, but he says it is so long since he left that they have forgotten all about him." Here the speaker was interrupted by another fit of coughing.

"No," she resumed, "he never even wrote to England to tell his friends when we were married. He was only a boy when he left home, and he was a good many years in Canady before he came over to the States."

Just at this point it seemed to occur to Mrs. Randall that she was talking rather freely about her husband to a person whom she did not know, and she pulled herself up with a rather short turn. She looked intently into her visitor's face for a moment, as though with an inward monition that something was wrong.

"But," she resumed, after a brief pause, "do you know my husband? I can't remember as I ever seen you before. You don't live in New York: I can see that. I guess you come from the West."

Then Mrs. Savareen felt that some explanation was necessary. She fairly took the animal by the extreme tip of his horns.

"Yes," she responded, "I live in the West, and I have only been in New York a very short time. I accidentally heard that Mr. Randall lived here, and I wish to ascertain if he is the same gentleman I once knew in Canada. If he is, there is something of importance I should like to tell him. Would you be so kind as to describe his personal appearance for me?"

The woman again inspected her very carefully, with eyes not altogether free from suspicion.

"I don't exactly understand," she exclaimed. "You don't want to do him any harm, do you? You haven't got anything agin him? We are in deep enough trouble as it is."

The last words were uttered in a tone very much resembling a wail of despair. By this time the visitor's sympathies were thoroughly aroused on behalf of the poor broken creature before her.

She felt that she had not the heart to add to the burden of grief which had been imposed upon the frail woman who sat there eyeing her with anxiety depicted upon her weary, anxious face.

"I can assure you," responded Mrs. Savareen, "that I have no intention of doing any harm either to him or to you. I would much rather do you a kindness, if I could. I can see for myself that you stand in great need of kindness."

The last words were spoken in a tone which disarmed suspicion, and which at the same time stimulated curiosity. The shadow on Mrs. Randall's face passed away.

"Well," said she, "I beg your pardon for mistrusting you, but my husband has never told me much about his past life, and I was afraid you might be an enemy. But I am sure, now I look at you, that you wouldn't do harm to anybody. I'll tell you whatever you want to know, if I can."

"Thank you for your good opinion. Will you be good enough, then, to describe Mr. Randall's personal appearance? I have no other object than to find out if he is the person I used to know in Canada."

"How long ago did you know him in Canady?"

"I saw him last in the summer of 1854--about five years ago."

"Well, at that rate I've known him pretty near as long as you hev. It's more'n four years since I first got acquainted with him down, in Ole Virginny, where I was raised. Why, come to think of it, I've got his likeness, took just before we was married. That'll show you whether he's the man you knew."

As she spoke, she rose and opened the leather trunk in the corner by the closet door. After rummaging among its contents, she presently returned with a small oval daguerreotype in her hand. Opening the case she handed it to Mrs. Savareen. "There he is," she remarked, "an' it's considered an awful good likeness."

Mrs. Savareen took the daguerreotype and approached the candle. The first glance was amply sufficient. It was the likeness of her husband.

She made up her mind as to her line of action on the instant. Her love for the father of her child died away as she gazed on his picture. It was borne in upon her that he was a heartless scoundrel, unworthy of any woman's regard. Before she withdrew her glance from the daguerreotype, her love for him was dead and buried beyond all possibility of revivification. What would it avail her to still further lacerate the heart of the unhappy woman in whose presence she stood? Why kill her outright by revealing the truth? There was but a step--and evidently the step was a short one--between her and the grave. The distance should not be abridged by any act of the lawful wife.

She closed the case and quietly handed it back to the woman, whom it will still be convenient to call Mrs. Randall. "I see there has been some misunderstanding," she said. "This is not the Mr. Randall I knew in Canada."

In her kind consideration for the invalid, she deliberately conveyed a false impression, though she spoke nothing more than the simple truth. There had indeed been "some misunderstanding," and Savareen's likeness was certainly not the likeness of Mr. Randall. As matter of fact, Mrs. Savareen had really known a Mr. Randall in Millbrook, who bore no resemblance whatever to her husband. Thus, she spoke the literal truth, while she at the same time deceived her hostess for the latter's own good. Affliction had laid its blighting hand there heavily enough already. Her main object now was to get away from the house before the return of the man who had so villainously wrecked two innocent lives. But a warm sympathy for the betrayed and friendless woman had sprung up in her heart, and she longed to leave behind some practical token of her sympathy. While she was indulging in these reflections the infant on the bed awoke and set up a startled little cry. Its mother advanced to where it lay, took it up in her arms, sat down on the edge of the bed, and stilled its forlorn little wails by the means known to mothers from time immemorial. When it became quiet she again deposited it on the bed and resumed her seat by the table.

Mrs. Savareen continued standing.

"I am sorry to have disturbed you unnecessarily," she remarked "and will now take my leave. Is there anything I can do for you? I should be glad if I could be of any use. I am afraid you are not very comfortably off, and you are far from well in health. It is not kind of Mr. Randall to leave you alone like this. You need rest and medical advice."

These were probably the first sympathetic words Mrs. Randall had heard from one of her own sex for many a long day. The tears started to her tired eyes, as she replied:

"I guess there ain't no rest for me this side o' the grave. I haven't any money to git medical advice, and I don't suppose a doctor could do me any good. I'm pretty well run down and so is baby. I'm told it can't live long, and if it was only laid to rest I wouldn't care how soon my time came. You're right about our being awful hard up. But don't you be too hard on my husband. He has his own troubles as well as me. He hain't had no cash lately, and don't seem to be able to git none."

"But he could surely stay at home and keep you company at nights, when you are so ill. It must be very lonely for you."

"Well, you see, I ain't much company for him. He's ben brought up different to what I hev, an's ben used to hevin' things comfortable. I ain't strong enough to do much of anything myself, with a sick baby. I'm sure I don't know what's to be the end of it all. Es a gineral thing he don't mean to be unkind, but----"

Here the long-suffering woman utterly broke down, and was convulsed by a succession of sobs, which seemed to exhaust the small stock of vitality left to her. The visitor approached the chair where she sat, knelt by her side, and took the poor wasted form in her arms.

They mingled their tears together. For some time neither of them was able to speak a word, but the sympathy of the stronger of the two acted like a cordial upon her weaker sister, who gradually became calm and composed. The sobs died away, and the shattered frame ceased to tremble. Then they began to talk. Mrs. Savareen's share in the conversation was chiefly confined to a series of sympathetic questions, whereby she extracted such particulars as furnished a key to the present situation. It appeared that the *soi-disant* Jack Randall had made the acquaintance of his second victim within a short time after his departure from Canada. He had then been engaged in business on his own account as a dealer in horses in Lexington, Kentucky, where the father of the woman whose life he had afterwards blighted kept a tavern. He had made soft speeches to her, and had won her heart, although, even then, she had not been blind to his main defect--a fondness for old Bourbon. After a somewhat protracted courtship she had married him, but the sun of prosperity had never shone upon them after their marriage, for his drinking habit had grown upon him, and he had soon got to the end of what little money he had. He had been compelled to give up business, and to take service with anyone who would employ him. Then matters had gone from bad to worse. He had been compelled to move about from one town to another, for his habits would not admit of his continuing long in any situation. She had accompanied him wherever he went with true wifely devotion, but had been constrained to drink deeply of the cup of privation, and had never been free from anxiety. About six months ago they had come to New York, where he had at first found fairly remunerative employment in Hitchcock's sale stable. But there, as elsewhere, he had wrecked his prospects by drink and neglect of business, and for some time past the unhappy pair had been entirely destitute. The baby had been born soon after they had taken up their quarters in New York. The mother's health, which had been far from strong before this event, completely broke down, and she had never fully recovered. The seeds of consumption, which had probably been implanted in her before her birth, had rapidly developed themselves under the unpromising regimen to which she had been subjected, and it was apparent that she had not long to live. She was unable to afford proper nourishment to her child, which languished from day to day, and the only strong desire left to her was that she might survive long enough to see it fairly out of the world.

Such was the sad tale poured into the sympathetic ears of Mrs. Savareen, as she knelt there with the poor creature's head against her boson. She, for the time, lost sight of her own share in the misery brought about by the man who, in the eye of the law, was still her husband. She spoke such words of comfort and consolation as suggested themselves to her, but the case was a hopeless one, and it was evident that no permanent consolation could ever again find a lodgment in the breast of the woman who supposed herself to be Mrs. Randall. The best that was left to her in this world was to hear the sad rites pronounced over her babe, and then to drop gently away into that long, last sleep, wherein, it was to be hoped, she would find that calm repose which a cruel fate had denied her so long as she remained on earth.

Mrs. Savareen, it will be remembered, was a pious woman. In such a situation as that in which she found herself, we may feel sure that she did not omit all reference to the consolations of religion. She poured into the ear of this sore-tried soul a few of those words at which thinkers of the modern school are wont to sneer, but which for eighteen centuries have brought balm to the suffering and the afflicted of every clime. Moreover, she did not neglect to administer consolation of a material kind. She emptied her purse into the invalid's lap. It contained something like thirty dollars--more money, probably, than Mrs. Randall had ever called her own before. "Keep this for your own use," she said--"it will buy many little comforts for you and baby. No, I will not take any of it back. I am comfortably off and shall not want it." Then, with a final embrace, and a few hurried words of farewell, she stepped to the bedside and imprinted a kiss on the little waif lying there, all unconscious of the world of sin and sorrow in which it held so precarious a dwelling place. Her mission was at an end. She silently passed from the room, closing the door behind her.

CHAPTER XII.
STILL A MYSTERY.

At the head of the stairway she paused for a moment to collect herself before passing down and out into the street. What she had left behind her was of a nature well fitted to excite emotion, and her bosom rose and fell with a gentle tenderness and pity. But she had learned self control in the school of experience, and her delay was a brief one. Mastering her emotions, she walked steadily down the two flights of stairs, opened the front door for herself, and was just about to cross the threshold when a man entered. The light of the street lamp fell full upon his face. It was the face of the man whose mysterious disappearance five years before had created such a profound sensation throughout Western Canada. There was no possibility of mistaking it, though it was greatly changed for the worse. Five years had wrought terrible havoc upon it. The scar on the left cheek was more conspicuous than of yore, and the features seemed to have settled into a perpetual frown. But, worst of all, the countenance was bloated and besotted. The nose had become bulbous and spongy, the eyes watery and weak. The man's clothes were patched and seedy, and presented a general aspect of being desperately out at elbows. His unsteady step indicated that he was at least half drunk at that moment. He did not see; or at any rate did not take any notice of the woman who gazed into his face so intently. As he staggered on his way upstairs he stumbled and narrowly escaped falling. Could it be possible that this disreputable object was the man whom she had once loved as her husband? She shuddered as she passed out on to the pavement. Truly, his sin had found him out.

She had no difficulty in finding her way back to the hotel, without asking questions of anybody. Upon reaching it she conferred for a moment with the office clerk, and then passed up to a small general sitting-room where she found her father. The old gentleman was beginning to be anxious at her long absence.

"Well, father, I find there is an express for Suspension Bridge at midnight. I think we had better take it. It is now half-past ten. I have learned all I wanted to know, and there is no use for us to stay here on expense. But perhaps you are tired, and would like a night's rest."

"Found out all you wanted to know? Do you mean to say you have seen him?"

"Yes, and I never wish to see or hear of him again in this world. Don't question me now. I will tell you all before we get home, and after that I hope you will never mention his name in my presence. When shall we start?"

Finding her really anxious to be gone, the old man assented to her proposition, and they started on their way homeward by the midnight train. They reached Millbrook in due course, the father having meanwhile been informed of all that his daughter had to tell him. Savareen's disappearance remained as profound a mystery to them as ever, but it had at any rate been made clear that he had absconded of his own free will, and that in doing so he must have exercised a good deal of shrewdness and cunning.

The question as to how far it was advisable to take the public into their confidence exercised the judgment of both father and daughter. The conclusion arrived at was that as little as possible should be said about the matter. Their errand to New York was already known, and could not be wholly ignored. The fact of Savareen's existence would have to be admitted. It would inevitably be chronicled by the ***Sentinel***, and the record would be transferred to the columns of other newspapers. The subject would be discussed among the local quidnuncs, and the excitement of five years since would to some extent be revived. All this must naturally be expected, and would have to be endured as best it might; but it was resolved that people should not be encouraged to ask questions, and that they should be made to understand that the topic was not an agreeable one to the persons immediately concerned. It might reasonably be hoped that gossip would sooner or later wear itself out. For the present it would be desirable for Mrs. Savareen to keep within doors, and to hold as little communication with her neighbors as possible.

This programme was strictly adhered to, and everything turned out precisely as had been expected. Mr. Haskins reached Millbrook on his way home to Tennessee within a day or two after the return of father and daughter from New York. He was informed by the father that Randall and Savareen were identical, but that the family wished to suppress all talk about the affair as far as possible. He took the hint, and departed on his way homeward, without seeking to probe further into matters in which he had no personal concern.

It was hardly to be supposed, however, that the local population would show equal forbearance. Curiosity was widespread, and was not to be suppressed from a mere sentiment of delicacy. No sooner did it become known that the father and daughter had returned than the former was importuned by numerous friends and acquaintances to disclose the result of his journey. He so far responded to these importunities as to admit that the missing man was living in the States under an assumed name, but he added that neither his daughter nor himself was inclined to talk about the matter. He said in effect: "My daughter's burden is a heavy one to bear, and any one who has any consideration for either her or me will never mention the matter in the presence of either of us. Anyone who does so will thereby forfeit all right to be regarded as a friend or well-wisher." This did not silence gossiping tongues, but it at least prevented them from propounding their questions directly to himself. He was promptly interviewed by the editor of the *Sentinel*, who received exactly the same information as other people, and no more. The next number of the paper contained a leading article on the subject, in which the silence of Mrs. Savareen and her father was animadverted upon. The public, it was said, were entitled to be told all that there was to tell. Savareen's disappearance had long since become public property, and the family were not justified in withholding any information which might tend to throw light on that dark subject. This article was freely copied by other papers, and for several weeks the topic was kept conspicuously before the little world of western Canada. Nowhere was the interest in the subject more keenly manifested than at the Royal Oak, where it furnished the theme of frequent and all-but-interminable discussion. Not a day passed but mine host Lapierre publicly congratulated himself upon his acumen in having all along believed and declared that Savareen was still in the land of the living. This landlord shared the prevalent opinion that the family should be more communicative. "I haf always," said he, "peen a coot frient to Mrs. Safareen. I respect her fery mooch, put I think she might let us know sometings more apout her discoferies in New York." Scores of other persons harped to the same monotonous tune. But father and daughter submitted to this as to a necessary penalty of their situation, and by degrees the excitement quieted down. I am not prepared to say whether the stepmother received further enlightenment than other people, but if she did she kept her tongue between her teeth like a sensible woman. As for Mrs. Savareen herself, she consistently refrained from speaking on the subject to anyone, and even the most inveterate gossips showed sufficient respect for her feelings to ask her no questions. She held the even tenor of her way, doing her work and maintaining herself as usual, but she lived a secluded life, and was seldom seen outside her own house.

Thus, several months passed away without the occurrence of any event worthy of being recorded. The mystery of Savareen's disappearance remained a mystery still. But the time was approaching when all that had so long been dark was to be made clear, and when the strange problem of five years before was to be solved.

CHAPTER XIII.
COALS OF FIRE.

The gloomy month of November, 1859, was drawing to its close. The weather, as usual at that time of the year, was dull and sober, and the skies were dark and lowering. More than three months had elapsed since the journey to New York, and Mrs. Savareen and her affairs had ceased to be the engrossing topics of discussion among the people of Millbrook and its neighborhood. She continued to live a very secluded life, and seldom stirred beyond the threshold of her own door. Almost her only visitors were her father and brother, for her stepmother rarely intruded upon her domain, and indeed was not much encouraged to do so, as her presence never brought comfort with it. The little boy continued to grow apace, and it seemed to the fond mother that he became dearer to her every day. He was the sole light and joy of her life, and in him were bound up all her hopes for the future. Of late she had ceased to scan his features in the hope of tracing there some resemblance of his absent father. Since her visit to Amity street, *that* fond illusion had wholly departed, never to return. She had ceased even to speak to him about his other parent, and had begun to regard herself in the light of an actual widow. Such was the state of affairs when the humdrum of her existence was broken in upon by a succession of circumstances which it now becomes necessary to unfold.

It was rapidly drawing towards six o'clock in the evening, and the darkness of night had already fallen upon the outer landscape. Mrs. Savareen sat in her little parlor with her boy upon her knee, as it was her custom to sit at this hour. The lamp had not been lighted, but the fireplace sent forth a ruddy blaze, making the countless shadows reflect themselves on the floor, and in the remote corners of the room. To both the mother and the child, this hour, "between the dark and the daylight" was incomparably the most delightful of the twenty-four, for it was consecrated to story-telling. Then it was that the boy was first introduced to those old-time legends which in one form or another have thrilled the bosoms of happy childhood for so many hundreds of years, and which will continue to thrill them through centuries yet unborn. Then it was that he made the acquaintance of Little Red Riding Hood, Jack the Giant Killer, and the Seven Champions of Christendom. The mingled lights and shades from the blazing logs of hickory in the fireplace lent additional charm to the thousand and one stories which the mother recounted for the child's edification, and I doubt not that Jack's wonderful bean-stalk is still associated in Master Reggie's mind with that cosy little room with its blended atmosphere of cheerful twilight and sombre shadow.

A few minutes more and it would be tea time. It would never do, however, to break off the story of the Babes in the Wood just at the time when the two emissaries of the wicked uncle began to quarrel in the depths of the forest. The child's sympathies had been thoroughly aroused, and he would not tamely submit to be left in suspense. No, the gruesome old tale must be told out, or at least as far as where the robin redbreasts, after mourning over the fate of the hapless infants "did cover them with leaves." And so the mother went on with the narrative. She had just reached the culminating point when an approaching footstep was heard outside. Then came a knock at the door, followed by the entrance of Mrs. Savareen's father. It was easy to see from his face that this was no mere perfunctory call. Evidently he had news to tell.

"Something has happened, father," said Mrs. Savareen, as calmly as she could.

"Well, yes, something has happened. It is nothing very dreadful, but you had better prepare yourself to hear unpleasant news."

"It is that man--he has come."

"Yes, he has come to town."

"Is he at the door?"

"No, he is at my house. I thought I had better come over and tell you, instead of letting him come himself and take you by surprise."

"What has he come for, and what does he want?" inquired Mrs. Savareen, in a harder tone of voice than she was accustomed to use.

"Well, for one thing he wants to see you, and I suppose you can't very well avoid seeing him. He is your husband, you know. He knows nothing about the journey to New York. He has no means, and looks shabby and sickly. I shouldn't wonder if he isn't long for this world."

"So you didn't tell him anything about the New York trip?"

"No, I didn't exactly know what your views might be, and he looked such a worn-out, pitiful object that I held my tongue about it. I think you had better see him and hear what he has to say."

It appeared that Savareen had arrived at Millbrook by the 4:15 p.m. train from New York, and that he had slunk round by the least frequented streets to his father-in-law's house without being recognised by any one. It might be doubted, indeed, whether any of his old friends would have recognised him, even if they had met him face to face in broad daylight, for he was by no means the ruddy, robust, self-complacent looking personage they had been accustomed to see in the old days when he was wont to ride into town on his black mare. His clothes were seamy and worn, and his physical proportions had shrunk so much that the shabby garments seemed a world too wide for him. His face, which three months ago had been bloated and sodden, had become pale and emaciated, and the scar upon his left cheek seemed to have developed until it was the most noticeable thing about him. His step was feeble and tremulous, and it was evident that his health had completely broken down. He was in fact in a state bordering on collapse, and was hardly fit to be going about. His financial condition was on a par with his bodily state. He had expended his last dime in the purchase of his railway ticket, and at the moment of reaching his father-in-law's door he had been well-nigh famished for want of food. When a loaf of bread and some slices of cold meat had been set before him, he had fallen to with the voracity of a jungle tiger. He had vouchsafed no explanation of his presence, except that he felt he was going to die, and that he wanted to see his wife and child. As he was tired out and sorely in need of rest, he had been put to bed, and his father-in-law, after seeing him snugly stowed away between the sheets, had set out to bear the news to his wife.

There could be no doubt as to what was the proper thing to be done. Mrs. Savareen made the fire safe, put on her bonnet and shawl and locked up the house. Then, taking her little boy by the hand, she accompanied her father to the old house where, six or seven years before, the handsome young farmer had been in the habit of visiting and paying court to her. On arriving she found the invalid buried in the deep, profound sleep of exhaustion. Consigning her boy to the care of her stepmother, she took her place by the bedside and waited. Her vigil was a protracted one, for the tired-out sleeper did not awaken until the small hours of the next morning. Then with a long drawn respiration, he opened his eyes, and fixed them upon the watcher with a weak, wandering expression, as though he was unable to fully grasp the situation.

The truth found its way to him by degrees. He shifted himself uneasily, as though he would have been glad to smother himself beneath the bedclothes, was it not for lack of resolution. A whipped hound never presented a more abject appearance.

His wife was the first to speak. "Do you feel rested?" she asked in a gentle tone.

"Rested? O, yes, I remember now. We are at your father's."

"Yes; but don't talk any more just now, if it tires you. Try to go to sleep again."

"You are good to me; better than I deserve," he responded, after a pause. Then great tears welled up to his eyes, and coursed one after another down his thin, worn face. It was easy to see that he was weak as water. His long journey by rail without food had been too much for him, and in his state of health it was just possible he might never rally.

The womanly nature of the outraged wife came uppermost, as it always does under such circumstances. Her love for the miserable creature lying there before her had been killed and crucified long ago, never to be revived. But she could not forget that she had once loved him, and that he was the father of her child. No matter how deeply he had wronged her, he was ill and suffering--perhaps dying. His punishment had come upon him without any act of hers. She contrasted his present bearing with that of other days. He was bent, broken, crushed. Nothing there to remind her of the stalwart, manly young fellow whose voice had once stirred her pulse to admiration and love. All the more reason why she should be good to him now, all undeserving as he might be. Our British Homer showed a true appreciation of the best side of feminine nature when he wrote--

"O woman, in our hour of ease,
Uncertain, coy, and hard to please;
When pain and anguish wring thy brow,
A ministering angel thou!"

She rose and approached the bed, while her gaze rested mildly upon his face. Drawing forth her handkerchief, she wiped the salt tears from his cheeks with a caressing hand. To him lying there in his helplessness, she seemed no unfit earthly representative of that Divine Beneficence "whose blessed task," says Thackeray, "it will one day be to wipe the tear from every eye." Her gentleness caused the springs to well forth afresh, and the prostrate form was convulsed by sobs. She sat by his side on the bed, and staunched the miniature flood with a tender touch. By-and-by calm returned, and he sank into a profound and apparently dreamless sleep.

When he again awoke it was broad daylight. The first object on which his eyes rested was the patient watcher who had never left her post the whole night long, and who still sat in an armchair at his bedside, ready to minister to his comfort. As soon as she perceived that he was awake she approached and took his wasted hand in her own. He gazed steadily in her face, but could find no words to speak.

"You are rested now, are you not?" she murmured, scarcely above her breath.

After a while he found his voice and asked how long he had slept. Being enlightened on the point, he expressed his belief that it was time for him to rise.

"Not yet," was the response; "you shall have your breakfast first, and then it will be time enough to think about getting up. I forbid you to talk until you have had something to eat," she added, playfully. "Lie still for a few minutes, while I go and see about a cup of tea." And so saying she left him to himself.

Presently she returned, bearing a tray and eatables. She quietly raised him to a sitting posture, and placed a large soft pillow at his back. He submitted to her ministrations like a child. It was long since he had been tended with such care, and the position doubtless seemed a little strange to him. After drinking a cup of tea and eating several morsels of the good things set before him he evidently felt refreshed. His eyes lost somewhat of their lack-lustre air of confirmed invalidism, and his voice regained a measure of its natural tone. When he attempted to rise and dress himself, however, he betrayed such a degree of bodily feebleness that his wife forbade him to make further exertions. He yielded to her importunities, and remained in bed, which was manifestly the best place for him. He was pestered by no unnecessary questions to account for his presence, Mrs. Savareen rightly considering that it was for him to volunteer any explanations he might have to make whenever he felt equal to the task.

After a while his little boy was brought in to see the father of whom he dimly remembered to have heard. His presence moved the sick man to further exhibitions of tearful sensibility, but seemed, on the whole, to have a salutary effect. Long absence and a vagabond life had not quenched the paternal instinct, and the little fellow was caressed with a fervor too genuine to admit of the possibility of its being assumed. Master Reggie received these ebullitions of affection without much corresponding demonstrativeness. He could not be expected to feel any vehement adoration for one whom he had never seen since his earliest babyhood, and whose very name for some months past had been permitted to sink out of sight. His artless prattle, however, was grateful in the ears of his father, who looked and listened as if entranced by sweet strains of music. His wasted--worse than wasted--past seemed to rise before him, as the child's accents fell softly upon his ear, and he seemed to realize more than ever how much he had thrown away.

In the course of the forenoon Mrs. Savareen's stepmother took her place in the sick chamber, and she herself withdrew to another room to take the rest of which she was by this time sorely in need. The invalid would not assent to the proposal to call in a physician. He declared that he was only dead tired, and that rest and quiet would soon restore him without medicine, in so far as any restoration was possible. And so the day passed by.

In the evening the wife again took her place at the bedside, and she had not been there long ere her husband voluntarily began his chapter of explanations. His story was a strange one, but there was no room to doubt the truth of any portion of it.

CHAPTER XIV.
THE BAD HALF CROWN.

He began by comparing himself to the bad half-crown, which always finds its way back, but which has no right to expect a warm welcome on its return. "Were it not," said he, "that I feel myself to be pretty near the end of my earth's journey, I could not have the face to tell you my story at all. But I feel that I am worn out, and don't think it likely that I shall ever leave this room except for the grave. You shall know everything, even more fully than I have ever known it myself until within the last few hours. They say that when a man is nearing his end he sees more clearly than at any other time of his life. For my part I now see for the first time that I have never been anything but a worthless lout from my cradle. I have never been fit to walk alone, and if health and strength were to come back to me I should not be one whit better than I have hitherto been. I don't know whether I ever told you that I have a streak of gipsy blood in my veins. My grandmother was a Romany, picked up by my grandfather on Wandsworth Common. I don't offer this fact as any excuse for my conduct, but I have sometimes thought that it may have something to do with the pronounced vagabondism which has always been one of my most distinctive features. So long as I was at home in my father's house he kept me from doing anything very outrageous, but I was always a creature of impulse, ready to enter into any hair-brained scheme without counting the cost. I never looked a week ahead in my life. It was sufficient for me if the present was endurable, and if the general outlook for the future promised something new. My coming to this country in the first place was a mere impulse, inspired by a senseless liking for adventure and a wish to see strange faces and scenes. My taking Squire Harrington's farm was an impulse, very largely due to its proximity to Lapierre's, who is a jolly landlord and knows how to make his guests comfortable. I had no special aptitude for farm life; no special desire to get on in the world; no special desire to do anything except pass the time as pleasantly as I could, without thought or care for the future. And as I have fully made up my mind to make a clean breast of it, I am going to tell you something which will make you despise me more than you ever despised me yet. When I married you I did so from impulse. Don't mistake me. I liked you better than any other woman I had ever seen. I liked your pretty face, and your gentle, girlish ways. I knew that you were good, and would make an excellent wife. But I well knew that I had no such feeling towards you as a man should have towards the woman whom he intends to make the companion of his life--no such feeling, for instance, as I have for you at this moment. Well, I married you and we lived together as happily as most young couples do. I knew that I had a good wife, and you didn't know, or even suspect, what a brainless, heartless clod you had for your husband. Our married life glided by without anything particular happening to disturb it. But the thing became monotonous to me, and I had the senseless vagabond's desire for change. We did fairly well on the farm, but once or twice I was on the point of proposing to you that we should emigrate to the Western States. I began to drink more than was good for me, and two or three times when I came home half-sees over you reproached me, and looked at me in a way I didn't like. This I inwardly resented, like the besotted fool I was. It seemed to me that you might have held your tongue. The feeling wasn't a very strong one with me, and if it hadn't been for that cursed four hundred pounds, things might have gone on for some time longer. Of course I kept all this to myself, for I was at least sensible enough to feel ashamed of my want of purpose, and knew that I deserved to be horsewhipped for not caring more for you and baby.

"The legacy from my father, if properly used, would have placed us on our feet. With a farm of my own, I might reasonably hope to become a man of more importance in our community than I had been. For a time this was the only side of the picture that presented itself to my mind. I began to contemplate myself as a landed proprietor, and the contemplation was pleasant enough. I bought the farm from Squire Harrington in good faith, and with no other intention than to carry out the transaction. When I left home on the morning of that 17th of July, I had no more intention of absconding than I now have of running for Parliament. The idea never so much as entered my mind. The morning was wet, and it seemed likely that we should have a rainy day. I was in a more loaferish mood than usual, and thought I might as well ride to town to pass the time. The hired man, whose name I have forgotten, was not within call at the moment, so I went out to the stable to saddle Black Bess for myself. Then I found that the inner front padding of the saddle had been torn by rats during the night, and that the metal plate was exposed. To use it in that state would have galled the mare's back, and it was necessary to place something beneath it. I looked about me in the stable, but saw nothing suitable, so I returned into the house to get some kind of an old cloth for the purpose. If you had been there I should have asked for what I wanted, but you were not to be seen, and when I called out your name you did not answer. Then, in a fit of momentary stupid petulance, I went into the front bedroom, opened my trunk, and took out the first thing that came uppermost. I should have taken and used it for what I wanted just then, even if it had been a silk dress or petticoat; but it happened to be a coat of my own. I took it out to the stable, placed it under the saddle, and rode off. Before reaching the front gate I saw how it was that you had not answered my call, for, as you doubtless remember, you were out in the orchard with baby in your arms, at some distance from the house. I nodded to you as I rode past, little thinking that years would elapse before I should see you again.

"I suppose you know all about how I spent the day. I had a bit of a quarrel with the clerk at the bank, and that put me out of humor. I had not intended to draw the money, but to leave it on deposit till next morning.

"Shuttleworth's ill-tempered remarks nettled me. I took the notes in a huff, and left the bank with them in my pocket. I ought to have had sense enough to ride home at once, but I went to the Peacock and muddled myself with drink. I felt elated at having such a large sum of money about me, and carried on like a fool and a sot all afternoon. I didn't start for home till a few minutes before dark. Up to that moment the idea of clearing out had never presented itself to my mind. But as I cantered along the quiet road I began to think what a good time I could have with four hundred pounds in my pocket, in some far-off place where I was not known, and where I should be free from incumbrances of every kind.

"In the half-befuddled condition in which I then was, the idea quickly took possession of my stupid imagination. I rode along, however, without coming to any fixed determination, till I reached Jonathan Perry's toll-gate. I exchanged a few words with him, and then resumed my journey. Suddenly it flashed upon me that, if I was really going to make a strike for it, nothing was to be gained by delaying my flight. What was the use of going home? If I ever got there I should probably be unable to summon up sufficient resolution to go at all. Just then I heard the sound of a horse's feet advancing rapidly down the road. An impulse seized me to get out of the way. But to do this was not easy. There was a shallow ditch along each side of the road, and the fence was too high for a leap. Before I could let down the rails and betake myself to the fields the horseman would be on the spot. As I cast rapid glances this way and that, I came in front of the gateway of the lane leading down by the side of Stolliver's house to his barnyard. As it happened, the gate was open. On came the horse clattering down the road, and not a second was to be lost if I wished to remain unseen. I rode in, dismounted, shut to the gate, and led my mare a few yards down the lane to an overhanging black cherry tree, beneath which I ensconced myself. Scarcely had I taken up my position there when the horse and his rider passed at a swift trot down the road. It was too dark for me to tell at that distance who the rider was, but, as you shall hear, I soon found out. I stood still and silent, with my hand on Bess's mane, cogitating what to do next. While I did so, Stolliver's front door opened, and he and his boys walked out to the front fence, where the old man lighted his pipe. Then I heard the horse and his rider coming back up the road from the tollgate. In another moment the rider drew up and began to talk to Stolliver. I listened with breathless attention, and heard every word of the conversation, which related to myself. I feared that Bess would neigh or paw the ground, in which case the attention of the speakers would have been drawn to my whereabouts. But, as my cursed fate would have it, the mare made no demonstration of any kind, and I was completely hidden from view by the darkness and also by the foliage of the cherry tree under which I stood. The horseman, as you probably know, was Lapierre, who had been despatched by you to bring me home. This proceeding on your part I regarded, in my then frame of mind, in the light of an indignity. A pretty thing, truly, if I was to be treated as though I was unable to take care of myself, and if my own wife was to send people to hunt for me about the neighborhood! I waited in silence till Lapierre had paid his second visit to the toll-gate and ridden off homewards. Still I waited, until old Stolliver and his boys returned into the house. Then I led the mare as softly as I could down the lane, and around to the back of the barn, where we were safe from observation.

"I chuckled with insane glee at having eluded Lapierre, and then I determined on a course of action. Like the egotistical villain I was, I had no more regard for your feelings than if you had been a stick or a stone. You should never suspect that I had wilfully deserted you, and should be made to believe that I had been murdered. Having formed my plans, I led the mare along the edges of the fields, letting down the fences whenever it was necessary to do so, and putting them carefully up again after passing through. I made my way down past the rear end of John Calder's lot, and so on to the edge of the swamp behind Squire Harrington's. Bess would take no harm there during the night and would be found safe enough on the morrow. I removed the bit from her mouth, so that she could nibble the grass, and left the bridle hanging round her neck, securing it so that she would not be likely to trip or throw herself. I showed far more consideration for her than I did for the wife of my bosom. I removed the saddle so that she could lie down and roll, if she felt that way disposed. I took the coat I had used for a pad, and carried it a short distance into the swamp and threw it into a puddle of water. I deliberated whether I should puncture the end of my finger with my jack-knife and stain my coat with the blood, but concluded that such a proceeding was unnecessary. I knew that you would be mystified by the coat as you knew quite well that I had not worn it when I left home in the morning. Then I bade farewell to poor Bess, and, unaccountable as it may seem to you, I was profoundly touched at parting from her in such a way. I embraced her neck and kissed her on the forehead. As I tore myself away from her I believe I was within an ace of shedding tears. Yet, not a thought of compunction on your account penetrated my selfish soul. I picked my way through the swamp to the fourth concession, and then struck out across unfrequented fields for Harborough station, eight miles away.

"The moon was up, and the light shone brightly all the way, but I skulked along the borders of out-of-the-way fields, and did not encounter a human being. As I drew near the station I secreted myself on the dark side of an old shed, and lay in wait for the first train which might stop there. I did not have to remain more than about half an hour. A mixed train came along from the west, and as it drew up I sprang on the platform of the last car but one. To the best of my knowledge nobody saw me get aboard. I was not asked for my ticket until the train approached Hamilton, when I pretended that I had lost it, and paid my fare from Dundas, where I professed to have boarded the train. I got off at Hamilton, and waited for the eastbound express, which conveyed me to New York."

CHAPTER XV.
REGINALD BOURCHIER SAVAREEN DISCOVERS THE GREAT SECRET.

Thus far Savareen had been permitted to tell his own story. I do not, of course, pretend that it came from his lips in the precise words set down in the foregoing chapter, but for the sake of brevity and clearness, I have deemed it best to present the most salient portion of the narrative in the first person. It was related to me years afterwards by Mrs. Savareen herself, and I think I am warranted in saying that I have given the purport of her relation with tolerable accuracy. There is no need to present the sequel in the same fashion, nor with anything like the same fulness of detail. The man unburdened himself with all the appearance of absolute sincerity, and made no attempt to palliate or tone down anything that told against himself. He admitted that upon reaching New York he had entered upon a career of wild dissipation. He drank, gambled and indulged in debauchery to such an extent that in less than six weeks he had got pretty nearly to the end of his four hundred pounds. He assumed a false name and carefully abstained from ever looking at the newspapers, so that he remained in ignorance of all that had taken place in the neighborhood of his home after his departure. Becoming tired of the life he was leading in the great city, he proceeded southward, and spent some months wandering about through the Southern States. His knowledge of horse-flesh enabled him to pick up a livelihood, and even at times to make money; but his drinking propensities steadily gained the mastery over him and stood in the way of his permanent success in any pursuit. During a sojourn at a tavern in Lexington, Kentucky, he had formed an attachment for the daughter of his landlord. She was a good girl in her way, and knew how to take care of herself; but Mr. Jack Randall passed for a bachelor, and seemed to be several grades above the ordinary frequenters of her father's place. Their marriage and subsequent adventures have been sufficiently detailed by the unhappy woman herself, during her conference with Mrs. Savareen at No. 77 Amity street.

The *soi-disant* Randall had gone on from bad to worse, until he had become the degraded creature of whom his wife had caught a momentary glimpse under the glare of gas lamp on her departure from the Amity street lodgings. The woman who supposed herself to be his wife had informed him that a strange lady had called and been very kind to her, but she had told him nothing about the lady having come from Canada. Why she was thus reticent I am unable to say with certainty. Perhaps it was because she attached no importance to the circumstance, after the lady's declaration that the daguerreotype did not represent the man whom she wished to find. Perhaps she had some inkling of the truth, and dreaded to have her suspicions confirmed. She knew that she had but a short time to live, and may very well have desired to sleep her last sleep without making any discovery detrimental to her peace of mind. Whatever the cause may have been, she kept silent to everything but the main fact that a kind lady had called and supplied her with a small store of money to provide for herself and the child. Savareen never learned or even suspected, that the lady who ministered to the wants of his victims was his own wife, until the truth was told to him by the wife herself. Small difference to him however, where the money came from. He had no scruples about taking a part of it to buy drink for himself and one or two loafers he numbered among his personal acquaintances. But there was sufficient left to provide for all the earthly needs of the dying woman and her child. The little one breathed its last within two days of Mrs. Savareen's visit, and the mother followed it to the grave a week later.

Since then "Jack Randall" had dragged on a solitary existence in New York, and had been on the very brink of starvation. Every half dime he could lay hold of, by hook or by brook--and I fear it was sometimes by both--was spent in the old way. Then his health suddenly broke down, and for the first time he knew what it was to be weak and ill. Finally he had been compelled to admit to himself that he was utterly beaten in the race of life; and with a profound depth of meanness which transcended any of his former acts, he had made up his mind to return in his want and despair, to the wife whom he had so basely deserted. Since leaving Westchester he had heard nothing of her, direct or indirect; but he doubted not that she was supplied with the necessaries of life, and that she would yield him her forgiveness.

It is possible to sympathize with the prodigal son, but whose heart is wide enough to find sympathy for such a prodigal husband as this?

His wife heard him patiently out to the very end. Then she told him of the arrival of Mr. Thomas Jefferson Haskins at the Royal Oak, and the consequent visit to New York. The recital did not greatly move him. The telling of his own story had again reduced him to a state of extreme exhaustion, and he was for the time being incapable of further emotion. He soon after dropped asleep, and as he was tolerably certain not to awake until next morning, there was no occasion for further attendance upon him. Mrs. Savareen drew to another apartment to ponder a while, before retiring to rest, on the strange tale which she had heard.

Next morning it was apparent that Savareen was alarmingly ill, and that his illness did not arise solely from exhaustion. A doctor was called in, and soon pronounced his verdict. The patient was suffering from congestion of the lungs. The malady ran a rapid course, and in another week he lay white and cold in his coffin, the scar on his cheek, showing like a great pale ridge on a patch of hoar-frost.

*   *   *   *   *

My story is told. The young widow donned the conventional weeds--"the trappings and the suits of woe"--prescribed by custom under such circumstances. It is only reasonable to believe that she sincerely mourned the loss of her girlhood's ideal, but it was surely too much to expect that she should be overwhelmed by grief at the death of one who had been practically dead to her for years, and whose unworthiness had recently been so unmistakably brought home to her. With her subsequent fortunes the reader has no concern; but it can be no harm to inform him that she remains a widow still, and that she at this moment resides with her son--a prosperous lawyer--in one of the chief towns of Western Canada.

www.bookjungle.com *email: sales@bookjungle.com fax: 630-214-0564 mail: Book Jungle PO Box 2226 Champaign, IL 61825*

The Codes Of Hammurabi And Moses
W. W. Davies

QTY

The discovery of the Hammurabi Code is one of the greatest achievements of archaeology, and is of paramount interest, not only to the student of the Bible, but also to all those interested in ancient history...

Religion   **ISBN:** *1-59462-338-4*   **Pages:132**
MSRP $12.95

The Theory of Moral Sentiments
Adam Smith

QTY

This work from 1749. contains original theories of conscience amd moral judgment and it is the foundation for systemof morals.

Philosophy **ISBN:** *1-59462-777-0*   **Pages:536**
MSRP $19.95

Jessica's First Prayer
Hesba Stretton

QTY

In a screened and secluded corner of one of the many railway-bridges which span the streets of London there could be seen a few years ago, from five o'clock every morning until half past eight, a tidily set-out coffee-stall, consisting of a trestle and board, upon which stood two large tin cans, with a small fire of charcoal burning under each so as to keep the coffee boiling during the early hours of the morning when the work-people were thronging into the city on their way to their daily toil...

Pages:84

Childrens   **ISBN:** *1-59462-373-2*   *MSRP $9.95*

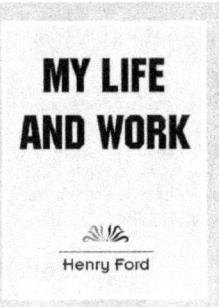

My Life and Work
Henry Ford

QTY

Henry Ford revolutionized the world with his implementation of mass production for the Model T automobile. Gain valuable business insight into his life and work with his own auto-biography... "We have only started on our development of our country we have not as yet, with all our talk of wonderful progress, done more than scratch the surface. The progress has been wonderful enough but..."

Pages:300

Biographies/   **ISBN:** *1-59462-198-5*   *MSRP $21.95* www.bookjungle.com *email: sales@bookjungle.com fax: 630-214-0564 mail: Book Jungle PO Box 2226 Champaign, IL 61825*

The Art of Cross-Examination
Francis Wellman

QTY

I presume it is the experience of every author, after his first book is published upon an important subject, to be almost overwhelmed with a wealth of ideas and illustrations which could readily have been included in his book, and which to his own mind, at least, seem to make a second edition inevitable. Such certainly was the case with me; and when the first edition had reached its sixth impression in five months, I rejoiced to learn that it seemed to my publishers that the book had met with a sufficiently favorable reception to justify a second and considerably enlarged edition. ..

Reference   ISBN: *1-59462-647-2*

Pages:412

MSRP $19.95

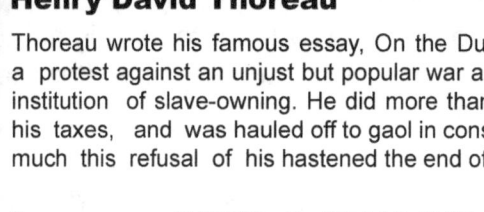

On the Duty of Civil Disobedience
Henry David Thoreau

QTY

Thoreau wrote his famous essay, On the Duty of Civil Disobedience, as a protest against an unjust but popular war and the immoral but popular institution of slave-owning. He did more than write—he declined to pay his taxes, and was hauled off to gaol in consequence. Who can say how much this refusal of his hastened the end of the war and of slavery ?

Law   ISBN: *1-59462-747-9*

Pages:48

MSRP $7.45

Dream Psychology Psychoanalysis for Beginners
Sigmund Freud

QTY

Sigmund Freud, born Sigismund Schlomo Freud (May 6, 1856 - September 23, 1939), was a Jewish-Austrian neurologist and psychiatrist who co-founded the psychoanalytic school of psychology. Freud is best known for his theories of the unconscious mind, especially involving the mechanism of repression; his redefinition of sexual desire as mobile and directed towards a wide variety of objects; and his therapeutic techniques, especially his understanding of transference in the therapeutic relationship and the presumed value of dreams as sources of insight into unconscious desires.

Psychology   ISBN: *1-59462-905-6*

Pages:196

MSRP $15.45

The Miracle of Right Thought
Orison Swett Marden

QTY

Believe with all of your heart that you will do what you were made to do. When the mind has once formed the habit of holding cheerful, happy, prosperous pictures, it will not be easy to form the opposite habit. It does not matter how improbable or how far away this realization may see, or how dark the prospects may be, if we visualize them as best we can, as vividly as possible, hold tenaciously to them and vigorously struggle to attain them, they will gradually become actualized, realized in the life. But a desire, a longing without endeavor, a yearning abandoned or held indifferently will vanish without realization.

Pages:360

Self Help   ISBN: *1-59462-644-8*

MSRP $25.45

The Rosicrucian Cosmo-Conception Mystic Christianity *by Max Heindel*　ISBN: *1-59462-188-8*　**$38.95**
The Rosicrucian Cosmo-conception is not dogmatic, neither does it appeal to any other authority than the reason of the student. It is: not controversial, but is: sent forth in the, hope that it may help to clear...　　New Age/Religion Pages 646

Abandonment To Divine Providence *by Jean-Pierre de Caussade*　ISBN: *1-59462-228-0*　**$25.95**
"The Rev. Jean Pierre de Caussade was one of the most remarkable spiritual writers of the Society of Jesus in France in the 18th Century. His death took place at Toulouse in 1751. His works have gone through many editions and have been republished...　Inspirational/Religion Pages 400

Mental Chemistry *by Charles Haanel*　ISBN: *1-59462-192-6*　**$23.95**
Mental Chemistry allows the change of material conditions by combining and appropriately utilizing the power of the mind. Much like applied chemistry creates something new and unique out of careful combinations of chemicals the mastery of mental chemistry...　New Age Pages 354

The Letters of Robert Browning and Elizabeth Barret Barrett 1845-1846 vol II　ISBN: *1-59462-193-4*　**$35.95**
by Robert Browning and Elizabeth Barrett　　Biographies Pages 596

Gleanings In Genesis (volume I) *by Arthur W. Pink*　ISBN: *1-59462-130-6*　**$27.45**
Appropriately has Genesis been termed "the seed plot of the Bible" for in it we have, in germ form, almost all of the great doctrines which are afterwards fully developed in the books of Scripture which follow...　Religion/Inspirational Pages 420

The Master Key *by L. W. de Laurence*　ISBN: *1-59462-001-6*　**$30.95**
In no branch of human knowledge has there been a more lively increase of the spirit of research during the past few years than in the study of Psychology, Concentration and Mental Discipline. The requests for authentic lessons in Thought Control, Mental Discipline and...　New Age/Business Pages 422

The Lesser Key Of Solomon Goetia *by L. W. de Laurence*　ISBN: *1-59462-092-X*　**$9.95**
This translation of the first book of the "Lernegton" which is now for the first time made accessible to students of Talismanic Magic was done, after careful collation and edition, from numerous Ancient Manuscripts in Hebrew, Latin, and French...　New Age/Occult Pages 92

Rubaiyat Of Omar Khayyam *by Edward Fitzgerald*　ISBN: *1-59462-332-5*　**$13.95**
Edward Fitzgerald, whom the world has already learned, in spite of his own efforts to remain within the shadow of anonymity, to look upon as one of the rarest poets of the century, was born at Bredfield, in Suffolk, on the 31st of March, 1809. He was the third son of John Purcell...　Music Pages 172

Ancient Law *by Henry Maine*　ISBN: *1-59462-128-4*　**$29.95**
The chief object of the following pages is to indicate some of the earliest ideas of mankind, as they are reflected in Ancient Law, and to point out the relation of those ideas to modern thought.　Religion/History Pages 452

Far-Away Stories *by William J. Locke*　ISBN: *1-59462-129-2*　**$19.45**
"Good wine needs no bush, but a collection of mixed vintages does. And this book is just such a collection. Some of the stories I do not want to remain buried for ever in the museum files of dead magazine-numbers an author's not unpardonable vanity..."　Fiction Pages 272

Life of David Crockett *by David Crockett*　ISBN: *1-59462-250-7*　**$27.45**
"Colonel David Crockett was one of the most remarkable men of the times in which he lived. Born in humble life, but gifted with a strong will, an indomitable courage, and unremitting perseverance...　Biographies/New Age Pages 424

Lip-Reading *by Edward Nitchie*　ISBN: *1-59462-206-X*　**$25.95**
Edward B. Nitchie, founder of the New York School for the Hard of Hearing, now the Nitchie School of Lip-Reading, Inc, wrote "LIP-READING Principles and Practice". The development and perfecting of this meritorious work on lip-reading was an undertaking...　How-to Pages 400

A Handbook of Suggestive Therapeutics, Applied Hypnotism, Psychic Science　ISBN: *1-59462-214-0*　**$24.95**
by Henry Munro　　Health/New Age/Health/Self-help Pages 376

A Doll's House: and Two Other Plays *by Henrik Ibsen*　ISBN: *1-59462-112-8*　**$19.95**
Henrik Ibsen created this classic when in revolutionary 1848 Rome. Introducing some striking concepts in playwriting for the realist genre, this play has been studied the world over.　Fiction/Classics/Plays 308

The Light of Asia *by sir Edwin Arnold*　ISBN: *1-59462-204-3*　**$13.95**
In this poetic masterpiece, Edwin Arnold describes the life and teachings of Buddha. The man who was to become known as Buddha to the world was born as Prince Gautama of India but he rejected the worldly riches and abandoned the reigns of power when...　Religion/History/Biographies Pages 170

The Complete Works of Guy de Maupassant *by Guy de Maupassant*　ISBN: *1-59462-157-8*　**$16.95**
"For days and days, nights and nights, I had dreamed of that first kiss which was to consecrate our engagement, and I knew not on what spot I should put my lips..."　Fiction/Classics Pages 240

The Art of Cross-Examination *by Francis L. Wellman*　ISBN: *1-59462-309-0*　**$26.95**
Written by a renowned trial lawyer, Wellman imparts his experience and uses case studies to explain how to use psychology to extract desired information through questioning.　How-to/Science/Reference Pages 408

Answered or Unanswered? *by Louisa Vaughan*　ISBN: *1-59462-248-5*　**$10.95**
Miracles of Faith in China　　Religion Pages 112

The Edinburgh Lectures on Mental Science (1909) *by Thomas*　ISBN: *1-59462-008-3*　**$11.95**
This book contains the substance of a course of lectures recently given by the writer in the Queen Street Hall, Edinburgh. Its purpose is to indicate the Natural Principles governing the relation between Mental Action and Material Conditions...　New Age/Psychology Pages 148

Ayesha *by H. Rider Haggard*　ISBN: *1-59462-301-5*　**$24.95**
Verily and indeed it is the unexpected that happens! Probably if there was one person upon the earth from whom the Editor of this, and of a certain previous history, did not expect to hear again...　Classics Pages 380

Ayala's Angel *by Anthony Trollope*　ISBN: *1-59462-352-X*　**$29.95**
The two girls were both pretty, but Lucy who was twenty-one who supposed to be simple and comparatively unattractive, whereas Ayala was credited, as her Bombwhat romantic name might show, with poetic charm and a taste for romance. Ayala when her father died was nineteen...　Fiction Pages 484

The American Commonwealth *by James Bryce*　ISBN: *1-59462-286-8*　**$34.45**
An interpretation of American democratic political theory. It examines political mechanics and society from the perspective of Scotsman James Bryce　Politics Pages 572

Stories of the Pilgrims *by Margaret P. Pumphrey*　ISBN: *1-59462-116-0*　**$17.95**
This book explores pilgrims religious oppression in England as well as their escape to Holland and eventual crossing to America on the Mayflower, and their early days in New England...　History Pages 268

QTY

The Fasting Cure *by Sinclair Upton*   ISBN: *1-59462-222-1* **$13.95**
In the Cosmopolitan Magazine for May, 1910, and in the Contemporary Review (London) for April, 1910, I published an article dealing with my experiences in fasting. I have written a great many magazine articles, but never one which attracted so much attention... New Age/Self Help/Health Pages 164

Hebrew Astrology *by Sepharial*   ISBN: *1-59462-308-2* **$13.45**
In these days of advanced thinking it is a matter of common observation that we have left many of the old landmarks behind and that we are now pressing forward to greater heights and to a wider horizon than that which represented the mind-content of our progenitors... Astrology Pages 144

Thought Vibration or The Law of Attraction in the Thought World   ISBN: *1-59462-127-6* **$12.95**

by William Walker Atkinson   Psychology/Religion Pages 144

Optimism *by Helen Keller*   ISBN: *1-59462-108-X* **$15.95**
Helen Keller was blind, deaf, and mute since 19 months old, yet famously learned how to overcome these handicaps, communicate with the world, and spread her lectures promoting optimism. An inspiring read for everyone... Biographies/Inspirational Pages 84

Sara Crewe *by Frances Burnett*   ISBN: *1-59462-360-0* **$9.45**
In the first place, Miss Minchin lived in London. Her home was a large, dull, tall one, in a large, dull square, where all the houses were alike, and all the sparrows were alike, and where all the door-knockers made the same heavy sound... Childrens/Classic Pages 88

The Autobiography of Benjamin Franklin *by Benjamin Franklin*   ISBN: *1-59462-135-7* **$24.95**
The Autobiography of Benjamin Franklin has probably been more extensively read than any other American historical work, and no other book of its kind has had such ups and downs of fortune. Franklin lived for many years in England, where he was agent... Biographies/History Pages 332

Name	
Email	
Telephone	
Address	
City, State ZIP	

☐ **Credit Card**   ☐ **Check / Money Order**

Credit Card Number	
Expiration Date	
Signature	

Please Mail to: Book Jungle
                    PO Box 2226
                    Champaign, IL 61825
or Fax to: 630-214-0564

ORDERING INFORMATION

web*: www.bookjungle.com*
email*: sales@bookjungle.com*
fax*: 630-214-0564*
mail*: Book Jungle PO Box 2226 Champaign, IL 61825*
or PayPal *to sales@bookjungle.com*

Please contact us for bulk discounts

DIRECT-ORDER TERMS

**20% Discount if You Order
Two or More Books**
Free Domestic Shipping!
Accepted: Master Card, Visa,
Discover, American Express